Zan's voice wa
passion.

'I can't wait to hav
in my life . . .'

Meeting Zan again was a strange enough coincidence, but that he should feel so strongly about her was incredible, almost unbelievable. Yet Annis had to believe it.

By some cruel twist of fate this man was back in her life and apparently intending to stay. Somehow she had to find a way of getting rid of him *now*. *Tonight*. Before this madness had time to grow and flourish . . .

Dear Reader

The new year is a time for resolutions and here at Mills & Boon we will continue to give you the best romances we possibly can. We're sure the year's books will live up to your expectations! This month we hope to shake off the winter chills by taking you to some wonderful exotic locations—Morocco, the Bahamas and the Caribbean. Closer to home, this is the time of year when we celebrate love and lovers, with St Valentine's Day. Which of our heroes would you like to spend the day with? Until next month,

The Editor

Lee Wilkinson lives with her husband in a three-hundred-year-old stone cottage in a Derbyshire village, which most winters gets cut off by snow. They both enjoy travelling and recently, joining forces with their daughter and son-in-law, spent a year going round the world 'on a shoe-string' while their son looked after Kelly, their much loved German shepherd dog. Her hobbies are reading and gardening and holding impromptu barbecues for her long-suffering family and friends.

Recent titles by the same author:

ADAM'S ANGEL

THAT DEVIL LOVE

BY

LEE WILKINSON

MILLS & BOON

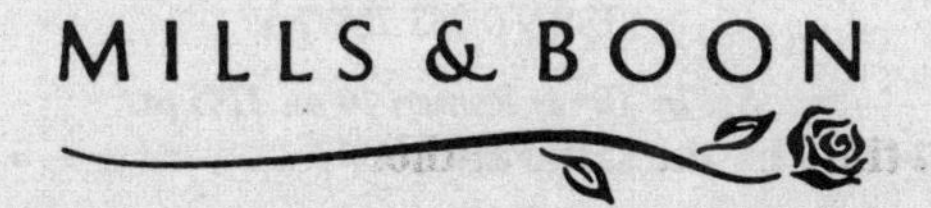

MILLS & BOON LIMITED
ETON HOUSE, 18-24 PARADISE ROAD
RICHMOND, SURREY TW9 1SR

First published in Great Britain 1994
by Mills & Boon Limited

This edition 1995

ISBN 0 263 78877 6

Set in Times Roman 10 on 11½ pt.
01-9502-53444 C

Made and printed in Great Britain

CHAPTER ONE

'I HOPE you didn't mind coming?' Stephen, sounding like an anxious schoolboy, broke into her abstraction.

Annis forced a smile. 'Of course I didn't. I'm enjoying it.'

He relaxed visibly, and she thought how sweet he was. Genuinely concerned about her. Easy to fool. With his light brown unruly hair and round toffee-coloured eyes, his chubby cheeks and lack of any waistline, he always reminded her of a big, cuddly teddy bear.

'Only you've seemed a bit quiet,' he pursued.

'Sorry, I didn't realise.'

Mentally isolated from the talk and laughter of a party to celebrate what had been described as a 'successful merger', she'd been thinking about Richard. Worrying about him.

'And you didn't eat much at dinner.'

'I wasn't very hungry.' That at least was the truth.

Giving up the attempt at conversation, Stephen asked a shade hesitantly, 'Would you like to dance?'

'Love to,' she assured him, getting up from her seat at the table.

She was slim and graceful, with the kind of cool yet stunning beauty that made men stare and women sigh with envy. Wanting to play down that beauty, she wore a simple black sheath, her only jewellery small gold hoops in her ears, a narrow gold bracelet circling her right wrist and a gold watch on a plain black strap on her left.

Her smooth silvery-blonde head, with its elegant chignon, held high, she preceded him on to the hotel's highly polished floor.

The band had started a quiet, smoochy selection, and as they joined the throng of dancers she found herself asking, 'How do you think this takeover by AP Worldwide will affect people's jobs?'

Damn! She hadn't meant to bring the subject up, but Richard had seemed so jumpy, so worried about his future prospects.

He'd poured out all his anxieties to her, rather than Linda, who, with fourteen-month-old twin girls to care for, was heavily pregnant with their third child.

'No one's quite sure yet,' Stephen admitted. 'But Power's a decent bloke by all accounts. Ruthless in many ways, but respected for being scrupulously fair, even generous to his employees, so long as they're on top of their job...'

So long as they're on top of their job... Her clear aquamarine eyes troubled, she repressed a shiver. Richard had confessed that, as far as work went, he was often out of his depth and relied heavily on Stephen to keep him afloat.

'It's not the kind of job I'm suited for,' he'd told her, miserably. 'But there's nothing else going at the moment so I've just got to grit my teeth and hope for the best. I can't afford to get the sack. The bank are threatening to turn nasty. We've a huge overdraft, and we're badly in arrears with the mortgage.'

She knew they had been having difficulties, but was shaken by the extent of them.

Making an effort, Annis thrust the memory of Richard's haggard face away and dragged her attention back to her companion who was continuing his panegyric.

'...He's only in his early thirties, and you don't get right to the top at that age without being ruthless.' Stephen, who was so downright *nice* it was a miracle he knew the meaning of the word ruthless, sounded admiring.

Annis sighed inwardly. There was a dull throbbing in her temples and she longed for the evening to end. As they slowly circled the edge of the crowded floor, she rested her head against Stephen's well-padded shoulder and made an effort to relax in his safe, undemanding embrace.

A moment later he was pulling away. Straightening.

Her back to the speaker, Annis heard a crisp, authoritative voice say, 'Good evening. It's Leighton, isn't it? Won't you introduce me to your guest?'

Surprised, flattered, childishly delighted to be noticed and have his name remembered by the great man himself, Stephen beamed and said, 'Annis, this is Mr Power, head of AP Worldwide...Miss Warrener.'

Annis, who had dutifully turned and extended a civil hand, stood without moving or speaking, shocked into immobility at the sight of the dark, dynamic man who wore his immaculate evening dress with such panache.

In a tough, unnerving way he was strikingly handsome. Unforgettable. There was no mistaking that well-shaped head of shorn black curls, no mistaking that lean, arrogant, strong-boned face. She *knew* it. *Hated* it!

'Zan Power,' he said, taking her hand in a light but far from casual clasp.

Zan. It *was* him! There couldn't be another man who looked like the legendary Jason and was called something as outlandish as Zan.

'Warrener——' He was frowning slightly, winged black brows drawing together over heavy-lidded eyes, the irises a dark green rayed with gold, brilliant against the clear, healthy whites. 'I know that name.'

'Richard Warrener, Annis's brother, works for you.' Stephen supplied the information. 'He's part of my team in the computer think-tank.'

There was a momentary flicker of surprise in those extraordinary eyes, which throughout the exchange had never left the perfect oval of her face. Then he was saying in his attractive, cultivated voice, 'Ah, yes. Isn't he here tonight?'

Once again it was Stephen who replied, 'His wife is having a baby quite soon. He didn't want to leave her.'

'That's understandable.' Still without removing his gaze from Annis's face, Zan Power went on with a politeness that in no way disguised the purposefulness, 'May I dance with your charming partner, Leighton?'

Displaying an unexpected firmness which earned her admiration, Stephen answered, 'That's really up to Annis, sir.'

'Well, Miss Warrener?' He held her gaze in a long, hard glance. There was no smile in his thickly lashed, feline eyes, no attempt to cajole, just a quiet waiting.

About to curtly refuse, she hesitated, remembering all she owed Stephen, then for his sake said a reluctant, tight-lipped, 'Of course.'

Half suffocated by the loathing that filled her, and an equally powerful feeling she was at a loss to identify, she moved into Zan Power's arms.

She was long-legged, tall for a woman at five feet, eight inches, yet still her eyes were only on a level with the cleft in his firm chin. Tense and awkward, she concentrated on keeping her body away from any contact with his.

He held her lightly, permitting the space between them, moving with a lithe grace that seemed strange in so big a man. The kind of grace one might expect to find in a gigolo, she thought with deliberate contempt.

Not a man willing to deal in polite platitudes, he asked, 'When you're not with Leighton do you always dance so stiffly, and in silence?'

'It depends who my partner is; how much I'm enjoying the occasion.' Her voice was cool, composed, belying the red-hot hatred that seethed inside.

They completed the circuit before he attacked from a different angle. 'Do you enjoy parties as a rule?'

'Yes,' she lied.

'But you've disliked every minute of this one.'

'What makes you say that?'

'I've been watching you.'

When, repressing a shiver, she made no reply, merely continued to move her feet and stare at his black bow-tie, he asked with a kind of wry curiosity, 'Why did you come tonight?'

'Because Stephen wanted me to.' She was aware, without even glancing at the man who held her so lightly yet so inescapably, that he was annoyed by her answer.

'And do you always do what Leighton wants?'

Goading the man who reminded her of a sleek black panther, she said, 'Whenever possible.'

'What is he to you? Friend? Lover?'

'So long as our relationship, whether it's merely platonic or more than that, doesn't disturb his work, I really don't consider that it's any of your business.'

Tawny green eyes caught and held aquamarine, his very look a threat. 'I intend to make it my business.'

'You surely can't want to control the lives of all your employees?' she protested incredulously.

'I don't.'

'Then what makes Stephen special?'

'*You* do.'

A sudden shiver of something closely akin to fear ran through her.

Softly, he went on, 'I won't tolerate anything other than friendship between you.'

'Won't tolerate...!' Anger mingled with alarm.

'So if by any chance it *is* more than that——' his face was steely, his mouth a hard line '—for everyone's sake I advise you to put an end to it at once.'

'You must be out of your mind!'

Ignoring her choked words, he added, 'However, I don't think it is. You have the look about you of a Snow Queen, as if no man has been able to melt the ice and turn you into a real woman.'

'I don't suppose it's occurred to you that a man might have *caused* that ice to form, made me—as you so fancifully put it—like a Snow Queen?'

'It hadn't,' he admitted seriously. 'But then I don't know you yet—in either the everyday or the old Biblical sense of the word.'

As her aquamarine eyes widened, he added with cool certainty, 'Though I fully intend to.'

Heart thudding against her ribs, she somehow dragged her gaze away. As well as angry, she felt scared, *threatened*. Which was ridiculous.

'I don't go in for casual affairs,' she said haughtily.

'A casual affair was the last thing I had in mind. I mean to have and to own you completely.'

The calm statement stopped her breath, as though a noose made of fear and fury had tightened around her slender throat.

But however much she abhorred and resented his brand of cool sexual arrogance, it could well hold a fatal fascination for some women.

Was that how he'd managed to bewitch Maya?

'No comment?' he queried, with a lift of one black, mobile brow.

Trying to hide how rattled she was, she said dismissively, 'I've already stated that I think you're insane, Mr Power.'

'Zan.'

'An unusual name.'

'My young sister couldn't say Alexander and, probably because it was less of a mouthful, her version stuck.'

'I presumed you'd chosen it specially to go with the image.' Before he could react to the taunt, she drew back and, lifting her chin, said disdainfully, 'If you'll excuse me now? I'm feeling rather tired.'

Turning away, she was about to leave him standing when his hand shot out and closed round her wrist like a steel fetter.

She froze into immobility.

Silkily, he said, 'I'll see you back to your table, Miss Warrener.' Releasing her wrist, he put a hand at her waist, his light, cool touch burning through the thin fabric of her dress like a brand.

Stephen rose to his feet as they approached, his brown eyes a little apprehensive, as if he half expected a ticking off for his guest's unsociability.

Instead, Alexander Power said pleasantly, 'I'll be in your managing director's office tomorrow morning at half-past eight. Come and see me there. You can give me a better idea of what exactly your team are doing. Goodnight, Leighton,' then, with a slight inclination of his black, imperious head, '*Au revoir*, Miss Warrener.'

Why that deliberate *au revoir*? she wondered apprehensively, as Stephen gazed with a kind of pleased awe after the tall, striking man making his unhurried way back to the top table.

Concealing her disturbed state as best she could, she asked, 'Would you mind very much if we left now?'

Stephen, who had been waiting for her to resume her seat, said with his usual good-natured compliance, 'Not if you want to go.' All the same, he looked disappointed.

Feeling guilty because she knew he was human enough to want to bask in the coveted glory of being singled out by the big boss, she explained, 'I've got a nasty headache.'

He peered at her. 'You do look rather pale.' Putting an arm around her waist—his clumsy concern in direct contrast to that other light but sure touch—he shepherded her towards the door. 'I'll fetch the car round while you get your coat.'

Though she refused to look in his direction, Annis felt Zan Power's predatory green-gold eyes fixed on her and an uncontrollable shudder ran through her slender frame.

As they left the sumptuous Piccadilly hotel and drove towards Belgravia, still on a high, Stephen marvelled, 'Fancy Mr Power remembering me! He's only seen me a couple of times, quite briefly. Of course he has a reputation for being a remarkable man...

'You'd never think it, to meet him now and hear him speak, but he came originally from the back streets of Piraeus, with a Greek mother and an English father.'

So he was half Greek... That accounted not only for Zan Power's looks but also for the almost imperceptible *foreignness* that lent such dark sorcery to his low-pitched voice.

But Stephen was going on, 'His mother died when he was about eleven and his father returned to England with the five children of the marriage. When he was barely eighteen his father was killed in an accident. The Social Services were going to split the family up, but he fought like a demon to keep them together.

'His brothers and sisters were all younger than him, but somehow he managed to support and educate them while he clawed his way to the top.'

Disturbed and agitated, unwilling to hear anything good about a man she detested, and aggravated by the open admiration, almost reverence, in Stephen's voice, Annis said sharply, 'If you've only met him twice, and briefly, I'm surprised he had time to tell you all that.'

Startled by her unusual irritability, Stephen explained sheepishly, 'He didn't tell me. One of the papers got hold of his life story. Zena Talgarth, the journalist who wrote it, described him as "a man's man but a woman's darling".'

She was probably in bed with him at the time, Annis thought acidly. Aloud, she remarked, 'I suppose cheap publicity and women fawning over him gives someone like Zan Power a kick... I feel sorry for his poor wife.'

Stephen shook his shaggy head. 'He's not married and never has been...'

Not married... Annis's silky brows, several shades darker than her hair, drew together in a frown. She could have sworn that Maya, in one of her last incoherent ramblings, had talked about a wife and family...

'...And according to the grapevine,' Stephen went on, 'he was furious about that newspaper article. He's a man who guards and values his privacy.' With a puzzled frown he added, 'You don't like him much, do you?'

'My, aren't you quick?' she said sarcastically.

Seeing Stephen's hurt expression, she was ashamed of herself. 'I'm sorry, please forgive me.' Then with magnificent understatement, 'No, I don't like him much.'

'You must have been the only woman at that party who wouldn't have willingly sacrificed her eye-teeth to dance with him.'

'If that's so, it's a pity he gave *me* the privilege.' Her tone was caustic.

'What don't you like about him?'

Unused to searching questions from Stephen, she hesitated before saying lamely, 'He isn't my type.'

'I should have thought he was any woman's type.' Stephen sounded envious.

She shook her head decidedly. 'He's too good-looking, too sure of himself. Far too brash for my taste.' Her voice rose a little. 'I hate the Don Juan type who——'

'He doesn't have that kind of image.' Looking a bit surprised by her vehemence, Stephen rushed to defend his hero. 'Matt Gilvary, his right-hand man, does, or rather *did*, before he became Mr Power's brother-in-law. They say he's steadied down since he was married... But though Zan Power's no saint,' doggedly Stephen returned to the point he was making, 'he's certainly no Don Juan...'

'Oh for goodness' sake can we stop *talking* about the man?' Annis burst out.

'I'm sorry...'

Instantly contrite, she said, 'No, I'm the one who should be sorry. I don't know what's the matter with me tonight.'

Then, wanting to make up for blighting her companion's happy mood, his pleasure in the evening, she added impulsively, 'It's just that I much prefer someone sweet and kind, like you.'

Thrilled at being compared favourably with a man of Zan Power's ilk, Stephen was still preening himself when, a few minutes later, they stopped in front of Fairfield Court, the three-storey brick building that housed Annis's ground-floor flat.

Knowing it gave him a kick, made him feel manly to cosset her, she unfastened her safety belt and waited until he opened her door and helped her alight.

As she stepped out on to the pavement a stylish silver BMW, which had been cruising a couple of cars behind them, drew up in a patch of shadow outside the block opposite.

Having crossed Fairfield's narrow, open frontage with its pair of leafless weeping willows, she opened the door while Stephen hovered by her elbow, his burgundy silk evening scarf hanging loosely around his neck.

Politeness forcing her, she asked, 'Would you like a quick coffee?'

'Love one,' he accepted cheerfully.

Ashamed, because she'd been hoping he would refuse, she switched on the light and led the way into a pastel-walled living-room which held the minimum of modern furniture.

In no mood for him to linger, she made a single mug of instant coffee, strong and milky and sweet, just how he liked it, and carried it through.

He looked surprised. 'Aren't you having one?'

'When I'm headachy, coffee only makes it worse. I'll have some cocoa when I go to bed.' And please let it be soon, she prayed silently.

Patting the empty place beside him, he invited, 'Why don't you come and sit by me and relax for a while? It isn't eleven yet.'

Carefully, she said, 'I know it's not late, but I'm feeling rotten...'

'I'm sorry... I wasn't thinking.' He downed his coffee in a few gulps and, scrambling hurriedly to his feet, made for the door. 'I'm nothing but a stupid oaf.'

'You're a dear.' In the open doorway she stood on tiptoe to touch her lips to his cheek.

His ears turning bright red, he pulled her into his arms and kissed her with clumsy fervour.

Though awkward, his kiss wasn't unpleasant, and she stood quietly in his embrace for a few seconds before gently freeing herself.

'I'll call you some time tomorrow,' he promised, and shambled to his car.

With the utmost relief, Annis closed the door and locked up.

Wanting only the oblivion of sleep, she hurried to get ready for bed, trying not to think of Zan Power. But, filling her mind with an overwhelming hatred, his powerful presence was there, all invasive, his darkly handsome face printed indelibly on her retinas.

As it had been since the first moment she'd set eyes on him more than three years ago.

Then he'd been responsible for destroying almost everything she'd held dear.

For months she'd been obsessed with thoughts of him and, harbouring a fierce need for revenge, had wanted him to suffer as he'd caused her and her family to suffer.

Her anger, her bitter animosity towards the man she'd caught only the one fleeting glimpse of had been so strong, so all-consuming, that it had taken her a long time to wake up to the fact that if she allowed such feelings to go on he'd end up destroying her too.

Making a valiant effort, she'd pushed him to the back of her mind, caused his image to fade, started to win the struggle to put the past behind her.

Until tonight.

Coming face to face with him again out of the blue had brought all the old torment and bitterness flooding back. Undone, in a split-second, everything she'd achieved in the preceding months.

It had also brought her a new and frightening anxiety. Was his stated intention to own her just some macho game? Or had she *reason* to feel afraid, menaced?

Her head was aching to such an extent that it was difficult to think clearly. But surely in the cold light of day his threat would just seem ridiculous?

She was brushing out the heavy silk hair which fell almost to her waist, gripping the brush until her knuckles showed white, when the doorbell pealed, startling her.

The thought that maybe Linda had gone into labour and Richard needed her to look after the twins sent her hurrying into the living-room.

Though surely he'd have rung her?

As she hesitated, she spotted Stephen's burgundy scarf lying on the settee, and picked it up with an exasperated sigh. The light was still on so he would know she wasn't yet in bed. Though why on earth he'd bothered to come back for it...!

A quick glance through the central peephole proved her conjecture right, providing a glimpse of white evening shirt-front and black bow-tie.

She pressed up the catch and unfastened the safety chain, but what she'd been about to say died on her lips as, shock exploding inside her, she gaped at the man filling her threshold.

Before she could make any attempt to collect her scattered wits he'd walked past her as if he owned the place and closed the door behind him.

Looming tall and decidedly dangerous, those amazing green-gold eyes with their thick sooty lashes fixed on her, Zan Power dominated the small room.

Tossing the scarf aside, she asked jerkily, 'What are you doing here? What do you want?'

His eyes holding hers, he smiled without answering. The irresistible allure of that smile and the certain knowledge that what he wanted was *her* threw her totally.

Panic-stricken, she cried, 'Get out! Go on, get out before I call the police.'

Raising narrow black brows, he stood aside so she could get to the phone. 'Call them, by all means. But what will you tell them? How will you justify such an extreme course of action?'

She stood, trembling in every limb, while her common sense told her she had lost her head and behaved stupidly, given him an added advantage.

Somehow she reined in the runaway panic and, slowly unclenching her hands, admitted, 'I'm afraid I over-reacted. But you took me by surprise.'

When he made no comment, just continued to stand and look at her, she added awkwardly, 'It's getting late and I was about to go to bed.'

She wished she hadn't said that when his eyes travelled assessingly over her fine Victorian-style cotton nightdress with its long sleeves and high neck, the smooth hair tumbling down her back like pale silk, the bare feet.

His inspection completed, he smiled mockingly. 'Don't worry, you're quite decent.' Then, briskly, 'I want to talk to you.'

Zan Power's voice, clear and low-pitched, with that very faint accent which lent it such devilish charm, sent shivers running up and down her spine.

Pressing slim fingers to her throbbing temples, she waited.

He indicated a chair. 'Won't you sit down?' It was an order in spite of the polite phrasing.

Clearly he intended the tête-à-tête...confrontation...whatever, to be on *his* terms.

Recognising the futility of trying to oppose him, she sat down, deliberately choosing a different chair.

Amusement flickered briefly in the tawny eyes, before he queried, 'Where do you keep your aspirin?'

She was surprised into answering, 'In the bathroom cabinet.'

'You haven't taken any?'

'No.'

Without a word he disappeared through the partly open door to return a few moments later with half a tumbler of water and two round white tablets, which he transferred from his palm to hers.

'I can tell by the tension in your neck and shoulders that you've got a headache.' Handing her the tumbler, he continued with wry humour, 'I could get rid of it with a few minutes' massage, but after your earlier reaction I hesitate to lay a finger on you, even for therapeutic purposes.'

Thank God for that, she thought fervently, swallowing the tablets. She couldn't bear the thought of him touching her.

For more than one reason.

Despite her hatred of him, like some beautiful but deadly snake he fascinated and attracted her. If he touched her...kissed her...she might be caught body and soul in his coils, unable to free herself ever again from that dark enchantment.

She shuddered.

Taking a grip on sanity, she pushed the fanciful notion away and told herself scathingly not to be an idiot.

'Do you mind if I sit down?' Without waiting for an answer, he took a seat opposite.

Unnerved afresh by his calm deliberation, the way his gaze never left her face, she said, 'You wanted to talk to me?' Then, with a sudden jolt, 'How did you know where I lived?'

Coolly he admitted, 'I followed Leighton's car.'

In her mind's eye she saw the sleek silver BMW glide out of the traffic stream and draw up opposite.

'So far as I'm aware it's not a criminal offence,' he added sarcastically.

Biting her lip, knowing she *had* to keep her composure, she said levelly, 'Perhaps you'll tell me why you went to so much trouble?'

'For several reasons.' He slipped a hand into his pocket.

As she gazed at him he reached over and clasped her right wrist, making her jump convulsively. 'I wanted to return this.'

Looking down at the gold bracelet he'd snapped on like a handcuff, she stammered, 'Th-thank you. I hadn't realised I'd lost it.'

'You didn't lose it,' he admitted coolly. 'I took it from your wrist.'

'Did you learn how to do that in the back streets of Piraeus?' The question was out before she could prevent it.

Just for a moment he looked nettled, then the anger was swiftly masked. 'I did, as a matter of fact. But though I and my brothers and sisters often went barefoot, our parents managed to feed us and keep a roof over our heads without the necessity for stealing.'

Staring at him with eyes that had turned darker and cloudy, she asked, '*Why* did you take my bracelet?' In spite of all her efforts her voice shook a little. 'You must have had a reason?'

'Oh, I had. Depending on the situation, I decided I might need an *entrée*, some legitimate excuse for knocking at your door.

'You see, I couldn't rest until I knew how things stood between you and Leighton. If he'd driven straight off, I would have let things ride until tomorrow, but when he came in with you I began to wonder if I'd been wrong in my assumption that you were no more than friends.

'Just as I was about to come over and break up whatever was going on, the door opened...' His voice soft but lethal, Zan added, 'When I saw him kiss you, I could have cheerfully broken his neck.'

Fear once again stifling her, she jumped up.

With one cat-supple movement he was on his feet and standing over her, his dark face only inches away from her own. 'I meant what I said, Annis. From now on I intend to be the only man in your life.'

'If you think after all you've...' Abruptly she halted the rush of bitter words, biting her inner lip until the lesser pain made the larger more bearable.

The past was best left alone. Nothing she, or Zan Power, for that matter, could do or say would alter a thing.

When she had herself under control, she carried on with icy composure, 'You don't seem to understand. There's no way I'd ever get to even *like* you.'

'I don't want you to like me. Liking is such an insipid, bloodless emotion. I want you to *want* me. To be as crazy for me as I am for you.'

Her heart racing with suffocating speed, she protested, 'You're quite mad.'

'I might be at that,' he admitted. 'But it's such a wonderful, exhilarating madness that I never want it to end.'

His voice roughened by passion, he went on, 'I can't wait to have you in my arms, in my bed, in my life...'

Then more quietly, 'But I won't try to rush you. I'll give you time to get used to the idea. All I want at the moment is a promise that from now on you won't see any other man.'

Meeting him again out of the blue was a strange enough coincidence, but that he should feel so strongly about her was incredible, almost unbelievable.

Yet she had to believe it. By some cruel twist of fate this man who had torn her whole world apart was back in her life and, apparently obsessed by her, intending to stay.

Somehow she had to find a way of getting rid of him *now*. *Tonight*. Before this madness had time to grow and flourish.

'I can't give you any such promise.' She tried to speak calmly, decisively. 'Apart from any other consideration, you were wrong in your assumption that Stephen and I are just friends. We've been lovers for some time now.'

Zan's olive-skinned face seemed to pale, the skin tightening over the strong bone-structure, as though her declaration was a knife she'd stabbed him with.

With a short, sharp sigh he echoed her earlier thought. 'Well, I can't alter what's happened in the past... But from now on you're *mine*. Don't ever forget that, Annis.'

Running his fingers into her silken hair, he took her face between his palms, and bent his dark head. His lips were firm and sure on her mouth, light, yet completely possessive.

She was still standing rooted to the spot when the latch clicked behind him.

Faintly she heard a door slam, an engine start, and his car draw away. But it was a long time before, moving like some zombie, she went to lock up and reset the safety-chain.

That fleeting kiss had shocked her to the core. Rocked her world. Nothing would ever be quite the same again.

Totally exhausted, she crept straight off to bed and fell asleep almost as soon as her head touched the pillow. But, though she slept, it was a shallow, restless sleep, haunted by a darkly arrogant face that both repelled and attracted her.

She awoke heavy-eyed and unrefreshed, that same face still effortlessly dominating her mind. Making all her hatred and anger surface. Bringing all the previous night's fear flooding back in a tide.

But she must try to keep a sense of proportion, she reminded herself sharply. Zan Power couldn't make her do anything she didn't want to do.

And perhaps he was already having second thoughts? After flaring up, his sudden passion might have flickered out, like a fire lit in the wrong place.

The best thing, maybe the *only* thing she could do was carry on as if nothing untoward had occurred, as if he hadn't turned her whole world upside down yet again, and see what happened.

Dressed in a smart charcoal suit and crisp white blouse, lightly made-up, her hair in its usual smooth chignon, she was almost ready to leave for work when the doorbell chimed.

Expecting the postman, she went to answer.

A young sandy-haired man wearing a green coat with 'Jay's, Florist' embroidered in red on the lapel said a cheerful, 'Good morning,' and, handing her a huge bouquet, went off whistling, despite the cold, grey day.

The long-stemmed, dark red roses, scented and velvety, were exquisite. Hot-house blooms like those must have cost a king's ransom, Annis thought dazedly. Stephen, bless him, had got carried away.

Nestling among the glossy leaves was a small envelope. Opening it, she took out the slip of pasteboard.

Written in a strong black scrawl on the gilt-edged card was one word. *Zan*.

Shock held her rigid for a moment, then, tearing the card in two, she dropped the pieces in the waste-paper basket as if they were stinging nettles.

Unable to bring herself to destroy the roses, after a moment's thought she picked up the bouquet and headed for the door once more.

Mrs Neilson, her middle-aged neighbour, was just getting about again after an operation, and Annis knocked most days to enquire if any shopping was needed.

None was this morning, but at the sight of the flowers Mrs Neilson's drawn face lit up. 'My dear, they're *beautiful*!' she exclaimed. 'How very kind of you.'

Wishing she could dispose of Zan Power as easily, Annis walked to the Tube station, girding her loins to face what a strange premonition warned her was going to be a fraught day.

CHAPTER TWO

JOINING the Friday morning rush, Annis caught a train to Oxford Circus then hurried the few blocks to her Regent Street office, a cramped first-floor room from which she ran Help, her own small temp business.

She employed ten women of diverse ages from varied walks of life, each with the willingness and ability to do several different jobs.

Requests for secretarial, nursing, housekeeping, cooking and catering help were the most common. But she and her staff could, and did, fill a variety of other roles.

Having unlocked the narrow, slightly shabby street door squeezed between a boutique and a video shop, she climbed the uncarpeted stairs and let herself into her office. Two wooden chairs and a desk were its only furnishings.

As she switched off the answering machine and hung her stone-coloured mac on a hook behind the door, the phone started to chirp.

A woman's businesslike voice identified herself as being from, 'Blair Electronics. Mr Blair's personal assistant...' and requested immediate help in the form of a competent secretary for the managing director.

Adding, 'I was advised to ask for a Miss Warrener, if she's available.'

'I'm Miss Warrener,' Annis said, and, a frown tugging at her well-marked brows, queried, 'But surely I haven't worked for you before?'

'No, but I understand you were highly recommended by the sales manager of one of our subsidiaries.'

'How long will you need my help for?'

'Miss Winton will be away for a month.'

All the details having been settled, Annis jotted down the address and promised, 'I'll be with you inside an hour.'

In a little over forty-five minutes, she was climbing the steps to the Marylebone office block which housed the electronics firm.

At the desk in the foyer she stopped to give her name and state her business.

'Turn right, then left,' the frizzy-haired receptionist told her, 'and you'll find the MD's office at the end of the main corridor. Go straight in, Miss Warrener. You're expected.'

Her heels sinking into the luxurious carpet, Annis made her way down the wide corridor. When she reached the unmarked door at the end, she knocked and walked in, as instructed.

Just inside the threshold she stopped short, feeling as though she'd received a punch in the solar plexus, as she saw the powerfully attractive face of the man sitting behind the leather-topped desk.

The shorn black curls, the green-gold eyes and bony, slightly crooked nose, the wide, thin-lipped mouth and cleft chin, were indelibly printed on her mind. If she never saw him again she would carry his hated image to her grave.

'Good morning, Annis.' A smile in those tawny eyes, he added, 'Close the the door and come and sit down.'

When she made no move to do either, he queried, 'Did you like the flowers?'

Somehow she found her voice. 'My next-door neighbour did.'

'So you gave them away?'

'What did you expect?' Without waiting for an answer, she rushed on, 'And I don't know what you hope to gain by dragging me here... I can't afford to play silly games. I've a business to run.'

'So have I. That's why I need a secretary.'

Trying to ignore the unnerving gaze fixed on her face, she demanded, 'How did you know where to find me?'

'Leighton was only too willing to provide any information I wanted. It was really quite amusing... But please do sit down.'

She shook her head. 'You've had your fun. Now I'm going.'

Softly, he said, 'I think not. We have a verbal contract. You agreed to work for me for a month.'

'The agreement was that I should work for the managing director of Blair Electronics.'

'Exactly.'

So this was yet another firm controlled by AP Worldwide.

Feeing the trap closing, she protested, 'Surely making me come here was just to prove how well you can manipulate people? You don't really want me to work for you...'

'Oh, but I do. Since having bronchitis just after Christmas, Miss Winton hasn't been at all well. I gave her a month's sick leave, so I require someone to fill her place.'

Annis's long-lashed almond eyes, beautiful eyes which slanted up a little at the outer corners, were blazing with anger and indignation. 'You mean you got rid of her on purpose!'

He moved his shoulders in a slight shrug. 'She needed a holiday. A few weeks' complete rest will do her a world of good.'

Reading Annis's mind with frightening accuracy, he went on, 'Of course I can't *force* you to stay. But you seem to be building up a nice little business, and if you value it you'd be wise to think carefully before doing anything rash.'

'That sounds remarkably like a threat.' Her voice shook a little as it was borne on her what power a man like him could wield.

'Merely good advice,' he said smoothly. 'After all, what's a month?'

As he spoke he got to his feet and strode over. A moment later he had closed the door, relieved her of her scarf and mac, and was ushering her to a chair.

It was done with such cool assurance that she was sitting down before she had time to weigh up what possible damage he could do Help if she ignored his 'good advice'.

Resuming his own seat, he observed, 'You won't find the work here too onerous. Apart from letters, all I need is someone to accompany me to meetings and take notes, and to act as my hostess if I do any entertaining.' Casually, he added, 'It will give you a chance to get to know me.'

'I don't *want* to get to know you,' she informed him icily.

'Then I'll have to see what I can do to change your mind... Now to business. I don't always tape-record——' he pushed a pad and pencil towards her '—so how's your shorthand?'

'Slow and inaccurate,' she informed him sweetly.

He laughed, as if genuinely amused, then, eyes gleaming devilishly, suggested, 'Well if you prefer, I'll settle for making use of your other talents.'

Biting her lip, she snatched up the pad and pencil.

They worked without a pause until twelve o'clock. His dictation was fast and decisive, giving no quarter, and she needed every ounce of her concentration to keep up.

All the same she was constantly and acutely aware of the man sitting opposite, *of how much she loathed and detested him*. Reluctantly aware also of his dark attraction, of the strong pull his magnetism had on her senses.

With a kind of horror she realised that if she hadn't had such *cause* to hate him, she might easily have fallen victim to his fascination. Might have found herself hopelessly infatuated with him.

As Maya had been. Maya—the one person Annis had really loved. Her life been a source of wonder to her, her death the greatest of pains. And she had died because of one man—Zan Power.

'Use my cloakroom if you want to wash and brush up before lunch.' His voice broke into her thoughts.

Looking up to meet those brilliant eyes, she said blankly, 'Lunch?'

'Yes. I want you with me.' She was about to refuse curtly, when he added, 'I have a luncheon appointment with Cyrus Oates, the American tycoon. As it's at his hotel, his wife will be with him.'

'I'm not dressed for lunching out,' she objected.

'You're dressed like the perfect secretary,' he assured her mockingly. 'Which is just as well, because after lunch I've a meeting at the bank, and I'd like you to take notes.'

She emerged from the cloakroom some five minutes later, hair and make-up checked, and they took the lift down to the underground car park where his silver BMW was waiting for him.

'What do you usually do for lunch?' he queried, when they were settled in the car.

'Buy a sandwich,' she told him, omitting to add that with high rents to pay both for her furnished flat and the Regent Street office it was all her tight budget would stand.

As they climbed the ramp to street level and joined the flow of traffic, he ordered, 'Tell me about your business.'

'I thought Stephen had given you all the information you wanted.'

Ignoring her prickly response, he asked, 'Do you usually work alongside your staff as well as coping with the administration?'

'Yes,' she answered shortly.

'But, being the boss, you can take your pick of the assignments?'

Oh, well, if he was determined to talk... And perhaps it *was* better than sitting beside him in strained silence.

'It doesn't usually work like that,' she answered a shade ruefully. 'I often get landed with the jobs no one else wants to do.'

Zan gave her a swift sideways glance and raised a black brow. 'Such as?'

'Well, there was taking care of George while the family went on holiday...'

'George?'

'A twelve-foot python. He turned out to be quite docile, not to say friendly. But feeding him proved a bit of a problem. The worst thing about pet snakes is they prefer their food on the hoof, so to speak. Have you ever tried making a very dead rat look alive?'

He was still laughing when they drew up outside the Farndale Hotel.

They were crossing the foyer when a large, balding man with rimless glasses and a paunch advanced on them. He held out a ham-like fist. 'Hello, Power. Glad you could make it. This is my wife, Dorothy.'

An equally large lady with eyes as pale as ripe gooseberries in a fleshy face, came forward with an outstretched hand. Having greeted the pair courteously, Zan said, 'May I introduce Miss Warrener, my secretary.'

'Pleased to meet you, Miss Warrener,' Cyrus Oates boomed, while his shrewd grey eyes assessed her slim figure, her cool, patrician beauty.

During lunch, while the men discussed business, Annis asked, 'Is this your first visit to England, Mrs Oates?'

The polite query was all that was needed to induce a flood of talk with the battering force of Niagara. A look of interest and an occasional word kept it flowing.

They were at the coffee stage, when with a suddenness that took Annis by surprise Mrs Oates finished an account of her visit to Harrods and said in strident tones, 'Gee, but your boss sure is good-looking. Don't you think he's handsome, honey?'

'I wouldn't describe him as handsome myself,' Annis said. Adding with a tight smile, 'Any more than I'd describe the north face of the Eiger as pretty.'

Her comparison went over the American's head.

'But don't you just *love* working for him?'

Annis caught a gleam of amusement in Zan's heavy-lidded eyes which made her aware he was following both conversations.

Evading the issue, she answered, 'I don't actually work for Mr Power. I'm only a temp.'

Overhearing the last few words, Cyrus Oates exclaimed, 'A temp?' Then to Zan, 'You don't get many secretaries look that good. Guess you won't want to part with her, huh?'

Catching Annis's eye, Zan said with smooth meaning, 'I shall certainly be taking steps to keep her with me on a more permanent basis.'

The subtle threat made a shiver crawl over her skin and her palms grow clammy with cold perspiration.

Lunch over, business matters apparently settled to everyone's satisfaction, they made their farewells and set off for the bank. It was nearly half-past four by the time the meeting was finished, and Annis, who had attracted quite a few curious and interested glances, was feeling stiff and tired. Though she was not normally prone to headaches, her head throbbed dully and the back of her throat was rough and dry.

Outside it was a bleak, prematurely dark afternoon, with more than a hint of snow in the air.

Turning the BMW into the traffic stream, Zan remarked, 'It's too late to go back to the office. I'll take you straight home.'

'Really, there's no need to go to all that trouble,' she said stiltedly. 'If you drop me at the next corner I can easily get the Tube.'

'It's no trouble.' His tone was quietly adamant.

After a pause, when the expected opposition failed to materialise, he asked, 'Have you lived at Fairfield Court long?'

'About three years.' She tried to hold at bay the hurt, the bitter memories crowding in on her.

'Do you like being there?'

'Not particularly.' The modern, characterless flat, with its small, square rooms, was functional rather than pleasing.

'Where does your brother live?'

Annis stiffened at the mention of Richard. Then, her voice as casual as she could make it, said, 'He and Linda have a house in Notting Hill.'

'Have you any more family?'

Like flicking a lighted match into a keg of gunpowder, that innocent question seemed to explode inside her head. She wanted to strike at him, to claw her nails down his handsome face, to watch him bleed.

Badly shaken by that flare of raw, primitive passion, the violence of her feelings, hands clenched into fists, she shook her head mutely.

Glancing at the frozen blankness of her face, Zan knew he'd hit a nerve. Though he didn't know how or why. There was so much about this woman that he didn't know. But he intended to.

When they reached Fairfield Court, Zan accompanied her to the door and waited while she unlocked it, but to her very great relief he made no move to follow her inside.

As she said a coldly formal, 'Thank you,' he stooped and touched his lips to hers in another of those light but proprietorial kisses that left her feeling as if she'd been caught in some terrifying whirlpool.

'*Au revoir*, Annis.'

A hand to her mouth, she watched him slide behind the wheel and drive away. She was still standing like a statue in the doorway when his car disappeared from sight.

Once inside she made herself a strong cup of tea, took a couple of aspirins and reviewed the catastrophic events of the day.

He'd managed so easily, so effortlessly to trick her into accepting the assignment at Blair's. But, hating him as she did, and frightened by the way each meeting added more fuel to her desire for revenge, she knew she couldn't go on working for him.

Anne and Sheila were both first-class secretaries, and on Monday, no matter what kind of upheaval it involved, she would send one of them in her place, and let him do his worst!

If he tried to ring her she would put the phone down, and if he came to her door she would refuse to open it. So long as she was careful, she would never have to see him again.

A hot bath alleviated some of her aches and pains and made her feel a great deal better. But, showing she was still very much on edge, she jumped when the phone shrilled.

'Annis?' Stephen's voice held a mixture of triumph and excitement. 'I've got tickets for *Malibu*, for this evening. I know it's short notice but you will come, won't you?'

'Well, I don't really...'

'I thought you'd be pleased.' He was instantly deflated.

'Any other time I would have been, only I don't feel much like going out tonight. In any case, I promised to be on hand this weekend to take care of the twins if Linda has to go into hospital, and I——'

'Before we left work I had a word with Richard,' Stephen broke in with plaintive eagerness, 'and he told me it might be several days yet before anything happens. Please change your mind... I'm sure it'll buck you up no end.'

Reminding herself yet again of just how much she owed Stephen, Annis forced herself to say brightly, 'You're probably right. Very well, I'll come.'

'Wonderful!' Once again he was bubbling over. 'I'll pick you up in about an hour.'

When Stephen knocked she was ready, resolved for his sake to at least *appear* to be enjoying herself.

'You look marvellous,' he told her, eyeing the simple, but elegant dress whose colour perfectly matched her eyes.

'Thank you.' She smiled at him, then asked, 'How on earth did you manage to get tickets for *Malibu*? I thought they'd been sold out for months.'

'You'll see,' he said mysteriously. Adding, 'I've a taxi outside, so we'd better get off. We haven't a lot of time.'

Why a taxi? she wondered. But perhaps he was intending to have a drink? Make the evening a festive one? Full of childlike pleasure and importance, he was clearly labouring under great excitement.

Only when they reached the theatre, and it was too late, did she realise why.

In the foyer, two people were waiting for them. A well-dressed woman with black curly hair and a superb figure, and the man Annis had promised herself she would never need to see again.

Coming face to face with him so unexpectedly gave her the same sensation as dropping in a high-speed lift, making her stomach clench and her heart begin to race with anger and alarm.

'Good evening, Miss Warrener... Leighton,' Zan said pleasantly.

'Sorry we're a bit late...' Stephen began.

Zan waved away his apology. 'I'd like to introduce Mrs Gilvary, my——'

'Don't be so formal, Zan,' the woman cut in with a teasing glance. Her smile friendly, she held out her hand first to Annis then to Stephen. 'I'm Helen, Zan's sister... How nice to meet you.'

As they were shaking hands the call bell went. Unable to think of any way out of the situation without hurting Stephen, Annis allowed herself to be ushered into the auditorium.

With smooth panache Zan placed her between the younger man and himself, remarking as he did so, 'I'm glad you were able to join us, especially as it's such short notice.' *Sotto voce*, he added sardonically, 'But then you told me you always try to please Leighton.'

Annis gave him an inimical glance. 'In this instance it was Stephen trying to please me.'

Catching the last few words, Stephen said eagerly, 'I knew you wanted to see *Malibu*, and when Mr Power said he had two spare tickets and suggested we join him . . .'

'You just knew I'd be *delighted*,' Annis murmured, the words holding an irony she was well aware the man on her far side had picked up.

Turning her head, she met those thickly lashed, heavy-lidded eyes with a cool challenge which almost faltered at the answering gleam which leapt into their green-gold depths.

In what she could now see was going to be a war of attrition, she would need every ounce of her fighting spirit, she thought, shakily. And was more than thankful when any further exchange was precluded by the lights going down and the orchestra breaking into a lively overture.

Living up to its notices, the musical proved to be bright and fast-moving. But though her eyes were fixed on the stage Annis took scarcely any of it in, all her attention, her awareness focused on the dark, powerful man beside her.

During the interval they had a drink in the bar and discussed the show. If Annis found little to say, no one appeared to notice.

Alternately hot and shivering, her limbs aching, her throat sore, she couldn't wait for the evening to end.

As soon as the final curtain went down to enthusiastic applause, with unobtrusive efficiency Zan shepherded them out ahead of the crush.

Demonstrating the effect of power and money, his car had been brought round and was standing by the kerb, a light drifting of snow beginning to settle on its shining bonnet.

When Stephen mumbled something about getting a taxi, Zan shook his head. 'You might have problems on a night like this. I'll drop you both.'

His tone brooked no argument, and Annis felt sure that had been his intention all along.

Only when she'd been handed into the front passenger seat did she fully appreciate the smoothness of the operation.

'Zan's marvellous when it comes to organising things,' Helen remarked, echoing her thoughts.

'That's how you get to the top.' Stephen's approving comment precluded the tart rejoinder Annis had been about to make.

'And stay at the top,' Helen added for good measure, making them sound as if they were forming the Zan Power Admiration Society.

As the two at the rear struck up a conversation, Annis, sitting silent and aloof beside the man who had always been her *bête noire*, puzzled over the situation. Dazzled by Zan and all he stood for, Stephen seemed to find nothing amiss in the way they'd been paired off, but it struck her as strange that Helen Gilvary, who was laughing now, showed no resentment at being relegated to the back seat.

Expertly threading his way through the late-night traffic, Zan addressed the younger man. 'I'll take Helen home first. You live at Knightsbridge, don't you?'

'That's right...' By the time Stephen had given him the exact location they were turning into Elwood Place, a quiet street in Mayfair lined with elegant houses.

When they drew up outside the porticoed entrance of number fifteen, Helen smiled and said a pleasant goodnight to them both before getting out.

Displaying his usual courtesy, Zan accompanied her to the door. When he bent his dark head to kiss her cheek, she put her arms around him and kissed him back with obvious affection.

It was a comparatively short drive to where Stephen lived. When he got out, with a reckless determination to rile Zan Annis followed him on to the snowy pavement.

Standing on tiptoe to touch her lips to his, she said, 'Goodnight, and thank you, darling.'

He looked as startled and delighted as a man who had come into riches beyond his wildest dreams.

When she got back into the car, Zan's face was as black as thunder. 'Fasten your seatbelt,' he ordered brusquely, and drove on, his mouth a thin, angry line.

Suddenly doubting the wisdom of her action, Annis leaned back against the head-rest and closed her eyes.

A finger flicking her cheek aroused her and she sat up, half stupefied, to find they were outside Fairfield Court.

'Where's your key?' Zan asked curtly.

Remembering his furious face when she'd kissed Stephen, she cravenly found herself wishing she hadn't deliberately provoked him.

'There's really no need for you to get out.'

Ignoring her uneasy protest, he made a swift search through her bag and located her key. 'Wait here.'

She followed him a moment later, shivering as soon as the wind whipped round her.

He turned on the fire and drew the curtains before helping her out of her silver fun-fur. Then, looming tall and dark and overpowering in the small room, he said coldly, 'I should put you over my knee for that little piece of bravado.'

'I don't know what you mean,' she muttered.

'You know perfectly well what I mean. I'm aware you only did it to annoy me, but you shouldn't have raised the poor devil's hopes like that, when it's obvious that you don't care a jot for him.'

'Well, that's where you're wrong! I *do* care.'

'Only in as far as it affects your brother.'

Seeing her freeze, he asked silkily, 'Did you think I wasn't aware how Leighton has been propping him up? Covering for him? It's common knowledge. I've known for weeks.'

Annis gazed at him with horrified eyes.

He smiled mirthlessly, and she found herself abstractedly noting the excellence of his mouth and teeth.

'I also know, despite the fact that he's a married man with a family, how you still tend to worry about him, mother him...'

'But how could you know?' she protested. 'Until last night you'd never set eyes on me.'

He shook his head. 'I saw you about three weeks ago. You came to Leighton's office when he was working late one evening. Then you walked out together and got into his car. I made some enquiries, found out who you were...'

Her heart missed a beat, then went racing on as she realised he'd spoken too casually to mean what she'd thought he meant.

'I hoped very much that he would bring you to the party. If he hadn't, I would have had to think up some other way of meeting you.'

Her head throbbing, her legs feeling as if they might buckle under her, Annis dropped into the nearest chair.

Studying the mauve shadows like bruises beneath her eyes, the translucent skin stretched tight over delicate bones, the faint dew of perspiration on her upper lip, Zan remarked, 'You look terrible.' Towering over her, he put a cool hand on her burning forehead. 'I think you're coming down with flu.'

She jerked away and muttered, 'Don't touch me.' Then, at the end of her tether, 'I wish you'd *go*. Leave me alone. Stay away from me permanently.'

His lips took on a wry slant. 'I can't stay away from you any more than I can stop breathing.'

Tilting her chin, he looked deep into her cloudy eyes. 'I intend to break down those defences, melt the ice you've surrounded yourself with, make you want me as much as I want you.'

There was a dark, brooding passion in his face, a relentless purpose that made her shiver.

'You're wasting your time,' she told him raggedly. 'There's no way I'll ever feel like that about you.'

Apparently unperturbed, he said, 'You already feel more strongly about me than you do about Leighton.'

She jumped to her feet. 'That's quite true. I'm fond of Stephen. *You I hate*. Now will you get out? I never want to see you again.'

'That might be difficult as you're working for me.'

'I'm not. Not any longer. If you really need help, on Monday I'll send you a competent secretary, but that's...'

The phone shrilled through her words.

Reaching out, Zan picked it up and answered with a brisk, 'Yes?'

After a moment he handed her the receiver.

She gave him a furious look and, taking a deep, calming breath said, 'Hello?'

'Thank God you're back...' Richard sounded distraught. 'I've been trying to get you for over an hour.

I'm at the General Hospital...' He made a sound halfway between a sob and a groan.

'What's the matter?' Annis demanded in sudden fear. 'Is something wrong?'

'Linda tripped and fell downstairs. She has a broken arm and there may be internal injuries... The shock caused her to go into labour, but they said it might be hours yet...'

Annis could have wept for her brown-haired, blue-eyed sister-in-law, pretty as a picture and not twenty-one until next month.

'Mrs Duffy is with the twins, but her husband works nights and she needs to get back to her own family.'

'I'll go straight over,' Annis said through stiff lips. 'Try not to worry too much. Everything will be all right, I *know* it will.'

Shaking from head to foot, she depressed the receiver rest, then released it again to call the taxi-rank.

Before she'd put in the first digit, Zan, who'd been standing close enough to hear both sides of the conversation, took the receiver from her hand and replaced it.

'What are you doing?' she cried. 'I need a taxi to get to Notting Hill.'

'I'll take you.'

'I don't want you to take me,' she cried fiercely. 'I don't need you or your help.'

'Don't be a fool, Annis,' he said shortly. 'You're about out on your feet.'

'I'll manage,' she declared stonily.

'You are the most stubborn woman I've ever met!' He turned off the gas fire, then dropping her coat around her shoulders fairly hustled her out of the flat and across the snowy forecourt to his car.

'Whereabouts in Notting Hill?' he asked, as he pushed her in and took his place beside her.

Feeling harassed to death, unable to fight any longer, she told him, and let him remove the safety belt from her fumbling fingers and click it into place.

Resting her pounding head against the soft grey leather of the seat, she prayed silently, feverishly, *please* let Linda and the baby be all right.

Despite her anxiety she must have dozed again, because when she opened her eyes they were drawing up outside the end-of-terrace villa that Linda and Richard had bought just before the recession sent house prices tumbling.

Snowflakes swirled around them, and her feet, inadequately clad in suede court shoes, were wet and cold before they reached the glass-panelled door.

A plump, dark-haired, flustered-looking woman in her middle thirties answered the knock promptly and exclaimed, 'Oh it's you, Miss Warrener! What a relief! They're both awake. You can probably hear them crying...'

'I'm sorry I've been so long getting here.' Annis's voice was croaky.

Mrs Duffy pulled on her coat. 'Well, now you are here I'd best be off. My own kids are ten and twelve, but I still don't like to leave them in the house on their own.'

'It's very good of you to have stayed so long,' Annis said gratefully.

'Can I take you home?' Zan offered.

Looking gratified, she said, 'Thanks, but I only live next door.'

The crying, which had temporarily abated, was resumed, rising to a crescendo as Annis hurried up the stairs.

When she reached the narrow landing, all at once feeling sick and light-headed, she staggered a little and was forced to lean against the nearest wall.

Zan's fingers encircled her wrist, keeping her there while he checked her pulse rate.

'Let me be,' she tried to shake off his detaining hand. 'I'm going to see to the twins.'

'You're doing nothing of the kind,' he corrected firmly. 'Firstly, you're not up to it——' while he was speaking he was opening doors '—and secondly, you don't want to risk them catching any infection.'

She could see the sense in that, all the same...

'Ah... this looks like the spare room.' He propelled her inside. 'Now you're going to get into bed and I'll bring you some hot milk.'

'But what about...?'

'*I'll* deal with the twins.'

And he probably *could*. He appeared to be able to deal with anything.

The combination of illness and emotional strain making her feel too spent to battle any longer, she stripped down to her undies and, climbing into bed, sat shivering.

In just a few minutes Zan returned carrying a couple of hot water bottles, and a tray with a beaker of milk and two red plastic feeding cups.

Having settled her with a hot water bottle behind her back and another at her feet, he put the beaker and two aspirin tablets on the bedside table before vanishing again.

She was just wondering anxiously how the twins would react to a strange man appearing in the nursery when, as if by magic, the crying stopped.

Sipping the hot milk, which had been liberally laced with brandy, she listened to the murmur of Zan's voice and thought bitterly how easy he seemed to find it to charm females of any age.

As soon as the beaker was empty she lay down, and within seconds was sound asleep.

Annis surfaced slowly and reluctantly to find her bedroom was full of snowy light. Only it wasn't her bedroom...

The events of the previous night rushed in like a tidal wave, and she sat up abruptly.

As soon as the room stopped spinning, she struggled out of bed and peered into the nursery. Both cots were empty.

Snatching a robe from behind the bathroom door, she went downstairs as fast as her shaky legs would allow.

No one was in the living-room, but a pillow and a neatly folded blanket suggested Zan had slept on the couch.

The smell of toast and coffee directed her to the kitchen.

Showered, shaved, immaculately—if a shade inappropriately—dressed, and clearly in command of the situation, Zan was putting boiled eggs into Beatrix Potter egg-cups.

Strapped in their high chairs, Rachel and Rebecca, models of rectitude, and as alike as two peas in a pod, contentedly spooned up their breakfast cereal.

'Hello, darlings.' Not wanting to get too close, she blew them a kiss.

Rachel, always the more solemn of the two, stared at her round-eyed, while Rebecca smiled and crowed and dribbled ground rice and apricots down her chin.

'Good morning.' Zan gave Annis a smile that stopped her breath as effectively as a silken noose. 'How are you feeling this morning?'

'Fine,' she muttered untruthfully.

He set a mug full of milky coffee on the table and pulled out a chair for her. 'You look as if you need to sit down.'

'First I must phone the hospital.'

'I've just been talking to them. Your sister-in-law is as well as can be expected. She's suffering from shock, but they don't think the internal injuries are too severe.'

Annis's pale lips framed the almost inaudible question, 'And the baby?'

'You've got a brand new nephew, born safely an hour ago.'

The relief was so great that Annis sat down abruptly and burst into tears.

A folded handkerchief was put into her hand.

While she dried her eyes and blew her nose, Zan added evenly, 'I've assured your brother that everything is all right at this end, so he's going to stay at the hospital... Now, do you feel up to some toast?'

Gulping the milky coffee gratefully, she shook her head.

'Then as soon as Mrs Sheldon arrives I propose to take you home to bed.'

'Who's Mrs Sheldon?'

'She's an ex-nurse and a very competent nanny. I've borrowed her from Helen, whose family, though still young, no longer really need her. She'll look after the twins for the time being.'

'But Linda and Richard can't afford a nanny,' Annis protested.

'That's all taken care of.' There was a knock, and he added, 'Ah, this sounds like her now.'

He returned after a moment or so with a neatly dressed, pleasant-faced woman in her forties.

When he'd made the introductions, Mrs Sheldon said cheerfully, 'Now don't you worry, Miss Warrener. I'll take care of everything.'

Feeling like death, Annis gave in and made her way upstairs to get dressed, recognising that even if she *could* manage to look after the twins it was in their best interest that she shouldn't.

But *someone* was paying Mrs Sheldon, and the very last thing she wanted was for any of her family to be in Zan Power's debt.

CHAPTER THREE

In less than half an hour Zan was escorting her into her own flat, and a few minutes later she was tucked up with a hot water bottle listening to him drive away.

After her earlier charged dealings with him, it had been almost an anticlimax when, brisk and practical, he'd said, 'Have a few days in bed. I won't expect you at work before Monday week.' Then, with a kiss as light as thistledown, 'Take care of yourself, Annis.'

She slept most of the day, and it was early evening when she was awakened by the phone.

'How are you feeling?' Richard's voice asked anxiously.

'Much better,' she assured him, and heard his sigh of relief. 'How is Linda?'

'A lot more comfortable, and the baby's doing well. He was nearly seven pounds and...' Richard filled in the details of his son's birth, before going on, 'It's such a relief to know that everything is being taken care of and I can stay with her. This nursing home is marvellous...'

'Nursing home?' Annis echoed blankly.

'Oh, didn't you know? Early this afternoon Linda was transferred to Carlton Heights private nursing home... The facilities are first class. There's a nice sitting-room and I've got a bedroom and en-suite bathroom...'

'But how can you possibly afford a private nursing home?' Annis asked dazedly.

'I don't have to. Mr Power's paying for everything. It was his suggestion. In fact he made all the arrangements, the same as he did over the children's nanny...'

Annis felt as though a bottomless pit had opened up at her feet. Urgently, she demanded, 'Have you stopped to wonder *why* he's doing all this?'

'It seems he's a philanthropist, especially where his staff and their families are concerned...

'He sent Linda a special delivery of flowers and said if there's anything she needs I only have to let him know. He's been absolutely marvellous...!'

When Richard finally finished singing his boss's praises, Annis put the phone down, filled with an apprehension that bordered on dread.

Zan Power, she was convinced, never did anything without a reason, and she couldn't believe it was a philanthropic one.

She spent the next few days quietly at home, eating scarcely anything, but taking flu-relief tablets and sleeping a lot.

Though she tried not to worry about the future, not to think about Zan, his dark presence was always there shadowing her mind, even while she slept. And she wondered dully if she would ever be free of him again.

She kept in touch with Carlton Heights by phone. Both Linda and the baby were making good progress and, using the nursing home as a base, Richard was now going in to work each day.

Every morning Zan sent fresh, passion-dark crimson roses, which she promptly gave away, but as though allowing her a breathing space he neither came to the flat nor phoned. For which small mercies she was truly thankful.

Discovering she was ill, Stephen rang and sent flowers but was with some difficulty dissuaded from visiting.

Sheila Collingford had taken over Annis's work. As well as organising Help, on Monday morning, as requested, she'd presented herself at Blair Electronics.

Much to her disappointment—'I really fancied working for a gorgeous hunk like him! Ooh, those *eyes*!'—Zan had politely but decidedly refused to have her, saying he'd wait until Annis was well enough to go in.

He'd have a long wait! she thought grimly.

Saturday morning, feeling almost herself again, Annis decided it was safe to visit Linda. She donned a smart black and white suit and, her blonde hair drawn back from her face, unconsciously emphasising the hollow cheeks and delicate bone-structure, sallied forth.

The nursing home was near St James's and, the weather having turned mild and sunny, she decided to walk.

Freshly opened daffodils and narcissus clustered in window-boxes. On the trees the first buds were about to burst, and along the fringes of the park drifts of colourful crocuses bloomed.

A well-spoken middle-aged receptionist directed her to the Warreners' flower-filled suite, which was on the ground floor overlooking a smooth expanse of green lawn.

Wearing a yellow frilly dressing-gown and slippers, her sister-in-law was sitting in an armchair by the window. Despite the plaster cast on her right arm, she looked so well that, temporarily forgetting her anxiety, Annis's heart lifted.

Smiling, Linda invited, 'Come and see your new nephew.'

Peering into the cot, Annis saw the baby was wide awake, dark blue eyes gazing up, tiny pink starfish hands waving.

A strange tug at her heart, she smiled mistily at the scrap and said softly, 'Hello there...'

Watching proudly, Linda remarked, 'He's already got a look of Richard, don't you think?'

Unable to detect any likeness to anyone in the crumpled baby face, Annis agreed nevertheless, and, taking a seat in one of the well-padded chairs, asked, 'What are you going to call him?'

'We thought Alexander...'

'Alexander?' Annis hoped her shock didn't show.

'Yes, after Richard's boss. He's been absolutely *terrific*, paying for all this...' she waved her good hand '...and Mrs Sheldon's wonderful with the twins...she brings them in every day to see me...'

Linda's blue eyes suddenly filled with tears. 'You can't imagine what a blessing it was to have everything taken care of. I just don't know how we'd have managed if Mr Power hadn't stepped in.

'Of course we've still got problems, but it was a great relief when Alex was born safely...and I'm making excellent progress now.'

'How long before you can go home?' Annis asked, trying to conceal her real feelings and sound in good spirits.

'A few days... I don't know for sure until the doctor's done his rounds.' The pretty face clouded. 'Only that's one of the problems. I may not have a home to go back to. You know we fell badly behind on the mortgage repayments? Well, we heard yesterday morning that the bank was going to repossess the house...'

Annis stared at her, the news like a hammer blow.

'Richard's been trying to find somewhere to rent. Somewhere we can *afford*, that is. And Mr Power's promised to see what he can do, but I don't hold out much hope...'

'O, ye of little faith...' The words were light and bantering, the low-pitched voice—with its slight but fascinating accent—one that Annis could have picked out from a million other voices.

Momentarily everything seemed to stop, her heartbeat, her breathing, her thought processes...

Then, like a swimmer who had stayed underwater too long, she dragged air into her lungs and felt her heart begin to pound with slow, heavy thuds.

Sitting perfectly still, her back to the speaker, she saw Linda's blue eyes light up with something akin to worship. 'Oh, Mr Power...'

'So how are you feeling today?' he asked gently.

'Quite a lot better,' she assured him. Then, to Annis, 'Mr Power calls in every day to see how I am.'

'How kind of him.' The cool words successfully disguised the storm of fear and hatred raging within.

Though Annis refused to turn her head and look at him, she was intensely aware of the tall figure standing close by.

'And you, Annis...?' His fingertip stroked the vulnerable nape of her neck in a brief yet possessive caress. 'How are *you*?'

Somehow she forced herself to answer, 'Up and about, as you can see.' But in her own ears her voice sounded hoarse and strange.

'Won't you sit down?' Linda asked, glancing from one to another, as though expecting to *see* the electricity that charged the air between them.

Taking the chair opposite Annis, Zan stretched his long legs with easy grace—Jason personified, with his shorn black curls, his lean, strong-boned face and cleft chin.

He was wearing a dark green polo-necked sweater and light beige trousers and jacket. It was the first time she'd seen him casually dressed, and he looked coolly elegant and hatefully attractive.

After studying the perfect oval of her face, he remarked, 'You've lost weight, and you're much too pale.'

In spite of all her efforts to the contrary, her gaze was drawn to his. The lick of flame in his handsome eyes set every nerve in her body quivering.

Needing to say something, she objected jerkily, 'I never have much colour.'

Softly, he said, 'Yet I can just imagine how you look with your cheeks flushed, your hair tousled and tumbled round your shoulders...'

As though he'd beamed the picture into her mind, she saw herself lying in his arms, eyes slumbrous, lips parted, feverish and breathless from his lovemaking. Wanting more.

Feeling her face grow hot, she moved uncomfortably, and glanced at her sister-in-law.

Linda was watching the interplay with a mixture of curiosity and startled comprehension that made Annis know she was presuming a deeper acquaintance, a relationship that didn't exist.

Something that Zan had *meant* her to presume.

As Annis opened her mouth to deny that impression, Richard hurried in, surrounded by an aura of energy and excitement.

When he'd greeted the two visitors—Annis warmly, Zan with respect—he went over to kiss his wife and take a quick peep at his infant son before dropping into a chair.

Tall and very fair, with clear-cut features and eyes of the same fascinating colour and shape as his sister's, his face hadn't as yet acquired the strength of character that made hers so much more than merely beautiful.

'I take it everything's gone smoothly?' Zan queried.

'Like clockwork,' Richard said eagerly.

'Then I suggest you set your wife's mind at rest without delay.'

A flush of exhilaration lying along his high cheekbones, the words tumbling over themselves, Richard rushed into speech. 'Mr Power has found us a super house not far from Hyde Park. It has four big bedrooms and a lovely light nursery, as well as a good-sized garden...'

The jubilant announcement filled Annis with dread. Once she'd seen a film of a tornado, seen how it sucked up and engulfed everything in its path. She'd been terrified of such destructive force.

Now Zan was taking over all their lives with the same deadly speed...

Through stiff lips, she demurred, 'Wouldn't the rent for that kind of place be way beyond your means?'

'Normally it would,' Richard agreed. 'But it's so exactly what we need and——'

'I own quite a bit of property in and around London,' Zan intervened smoothly. 'But Rydal Lodge was standing empty, and it seemed ideal for two reasons. It's nice and central and its accommodation includes a self-contained flat for a nanny.'

'But Linda and Richard won't have a nanny,' Annis said sharply.

Zan met and held her glance. 'Mrs Sheldon is more than happy to stay on.'

Before Annis could open her mouth to object, he added, his tone reasonable, 'There's no way Mrs

Warrener is going to be able to take care of a baby and the twins with a broken arm. Even when the plaster's off, she'll need help for a while at least.'

It was a fact. One that Annis was unable to dispute.

'That would have been marvellous,' Linda said shakily. 'I haven't dared think how I'll cope... But Annis is right, we can't afford either a place like that or a nanny.'

'Before you make up your mind, perhaps you should hear the rest of your husband's news?' Zan suggested, his expression bland.

As both women turned to look at him, Richard proudly announced, 'Starting Monday, I've got a new job.'

'A new job?' Linda echoed.

Flushed with success, seeming to grow in stature, Richard went on, 'I'm going to be in charge of public relations for the whole of AP worldwide, with a salary three times what it is at present... But, even more important than that, it's work I'm going to enjoy and, I believe, do well.'

After all the months of worry, it was so *wonderful* to see him look like that, Annis thought dazedly, if only this job was *genuine*. But she couldn't believe it was.

'How... when...?' Linda stammered.

It was Zan who answered. 'Richard wasn't happy with what he was doing, and for the past week we've been discussing possible alternatives...'

Looking as if the sky had fallen in on her, Linda whispered, 'I can hardly believe it.'

Richard took her hand and squeezed it. 'You'd better believe it.' Then to Annis, 'So you see, sis, we really *can* afford the house and a nanny, thanks to Mr Power.'

Sitting mute and helpless, Annis clenched her hands until the pearly oval nails dug deep into her palms. She wanted to scream a warning, to tell them he was a ruthless, unscrupulous man who had been largely responsible for Maya's death, and who was almost certainly trying to lure them into a trap.

But she knew with a kind of sick certainty that it would be no use.

Maya's death and the events that followed had been less traumatic for Richard—away at college, he had been deliberately shielded from the worst—and if challenged on that last melodramatic charge she might have difficulty justifying it.

Zan was so much in control, so adroit at juggling situations and people. He would smile and look unconcerned, mildly amused perhaps, and even if they believed there was *some* basis of truth, her accusations would sound absurd, blown up out of all proportion...

Turning brimming eyes on Zan, Linda whispered, 'How can we ever repay you?'

'When you're well enough to cope with guests you can invite us to dinner in your new home.'

His use of the word 'us' and the warm glance he gave Annis wasn't lost on the other two.

Oh, but he was an expert tactician! she thought bitterly, tacitly implying an intimacy that provided a credible motive for helping them.

'You'll be the first to come,' Linda promised. She sniffed and brushed away the happy tears. 'You said it was empty? If Richard could start making arrangements to move in early next week...?'

Gravely, Zan told her, 'I believe he has one final surprise for you.'

Grinning widely, Richard said, 'We moved in this morning, lock, stock, and barrel.'

Reeling from the shock, Annis realised grimly that she should have expected it. When Zan wanted something done he moved with the speed of a striking cobra and never left anything to chance.

Laughing at Linda's open-mouthed astonishment, Richard added, 'There were carpets down and curtains already up, which was a big help. By eleven o'clock all the furniture was in place, the last of the cartons had been unpacked, and the removal men were having a cup of tea prior to leaving.'

'How did Mrs Sheldon manage with the twins at such short notice?' Linda asked faintly.

'She took it in her stride. When I came away she was setting the kitchen to rights before getting lunch ready. And talking of lunch...'

Zan stood up in one fluid movement. 'Yes, it's time we were off. We have things to discuss.' He smiled down at Annis and, a hand beneath her elbow, urged her to her feet.

Picking up her shoulder-bag, she said her goodbyes like a programmed robot and accompanied him through the main lounge area and out into the sunshine.

His BMW was waiting on the gravel apron. Coolly in command, he opened the door and pushed her gently but firmly into the front passenger seat.

Whistling 'Oh, What A Beautiful Morning' half under his breath, he swung left at the end of the drive and joined the thronging traffic.

Thrown completely by the ambivalence of her feelings—relief at the change in Richard, and the easing of so much pressure; fear of how precarious his good fortune was and what the eventual cost might be—Annis struggled to regain her mental balance.

By the time she'd succeeded they were turning down Park Lane. 'Where are we going?' she demanded in sudden alarm.

His profile darkly austere, the thick sweep of curly lashes against his hard cheek only emphasising his arrogant maleness, he answered, 'Home.'

For some reason that monosyllable scared her. She shook her head. 'I want to go back to my own flat.'

His tone quietly adamant, he said, 'We're going to my place to have lunch, and talk.'

It was a battle of wits and wills in which he had the advantage. Knowing it was useless to argue, she relapsed into silence.

After a relatively short time they turned between high gateposts topped by a pair of fierce-looking stone guardians. The mythological creatures, with their eagles' heads and wings and lions' bodies, seemed singularly appropriate.

Griffin House was two-storey, L-shaped, substantially built, and charming, its creeper-covered walls, the mature trees and the privacy of its garden giving a country feel to it in the heart of London.

Zan opened the beautiful oak door, which was flanked by a pair of old carriage-lamps, and led her across a wood-panelled hall and into a large, period living-kitchen.

Curious, despite herself, unsure quite what to expect, it came as a total surprise to her.

It was a most attractive room, with a refectory table and a comfortable chintzy suite. Bowls of spring flowers stood in the windowsills and a glowing fire burnt on the wide stone hearth.

Perhaps because he seemed so very masculine—so dangerous and untamed, despite his veneer of sophistication—she hadn't thought of him as a man who would appreciate, or fit into, a cosy domestic setting.

An amused twist to his lips that suggested he knew precisely what she was thinking, he remarked, 'I've always preferred this room to the more formal sitting-room.'

When he'd added a couple of logs to the fire and stirred them into a blaze, he put a covered tray on the coffee-table, observing, 'My housekeeper always spends the weekend with her sister, who's an invalid, so it's a cold lunch on our knees.'

Her appetite virtually non-existent, Annis managed to force down a chicken sandwich and some salad. By the time she'd finished, the percolator was bubbling, the smell of freshly ground coffee filling the kitchen. When Zan had poured the fragrant brew, they drank in silence until, seated opposite, his brilliant gaze resting on her pale, tense face, he threw down the gauntlet. 'Well, Annis?'

She picked it up.

Her voice studiously calm and disciplined, belying the way her heart had started to race with suffocating speed, she asked, 'Are you expecting me to thank you for what you've done for Linda and Richard?'

'Were you planning to?'

'It depends on why you did it.'

He queried ironically, 'You don't believe it was out of the goodness of my heart?'

'No.'

'Then you know why.'

Oh, yes, she knew. She knew only too well.

Still she fought the knowledge, and said without inflextion, 'You've gone to a great deal of trouble and expense.'

His smile deepened laughter lines at the corners of his eyes and made grooves beside his firm mouth. 'I'm sure it will be worth it.'

'Don't bet on it,' she cried sharply. 'If you're hoping I'll be grateful enough to fall into your arms...'

Black head tilted to one side, he appeared to be considering the matter. After a moment, he said judiciously, 'I hardly entertained *that* hope.'

'Then what *were* you hoping for?'

He got to his feet and, as though purposely giving her space, went to lean against the mantelpiece. Gently, coaxingly, he said, 'A chance to start again, to make you dislike me less...'

'Watch my lips——' she saw his black brows draw together at the disdainful words '—and believe me when I say you're wasting your time. I'll *never* like you. Nothing you can do or say will ever alter that.'

His face tightened as though she'd struck him, and fury at her scornful rejection, although carefully controlled and unspoken, was as palpable as if he'd banged his fists on the mantel.

Full of blind hatred, and suddenly scared to death of the anger and hostility she'd aroused, she jumped to her feet and headed for the door.

Before she could open it, he reached a hand over her shoulder and held it shut. His voice like velvet-covered steel, he drawled, 'Don't rush off.'

'I'm going home.' She spoke with a great deal more assurance than she felt.

Flatly, he informed her, 'You're going nowhere. You're staying right here where I want you.'

She swung round, her back to the door. His dark, cruel face was so close that she could see a tell-tale pulse hammering in his temple, and a tiny, jagged scar just beneath his left eye.

A dew of fear broke out all over her body. Somehow she managed to say coldly, 'I don't take orders from anyone.'

'Not *anyone*. *Me*. From now on you're going to do exactly as I say.'

Her back pressed against the panels, she spat at him, 'You must be crazy if you think——'

'I don't *think*. I *know*.'

His quiet certainty shook her rigid. Still she defied him. 'I've no intention of either staying here or taking orders from you.'

'Don't you care what happens to Richard and his family?'

'You know perfectly well I care,' she burst out hoarsely.

'Then, in order to keep things running smoothly for them, you may need to reconsider.'

'What do you mean by that?' she asked unsteadily.

'Exactly what you think I mean. You see, having settled his overdraft and paid off all his other creditors, your brother owes me a great deal of money...

'If he does the PR job well and becomes a key man in my organisation—which I hope and expect he will—he'll have no trouble paying that money back.

'On the other hand, I might find he isn't right for the job after all, and that could create problems for him, especially if I decided to withdraw my support...'

'That's blackmail,' she breathed, aghast.

'You've rejected the softly, softly approach, so I'm afraid you leave me no alternative.'

Her aquamarine eyes turbulent as a stormy sea, she cried, 'You really are a swine!'

Zan smiled a shade thinly, wryly amused by her vehemence. Then, as though to bring home his absolute mastery, he moved away from the door and, indicating the chair she had just left, ordered with casual authority, 'Sit down, Annis.'

Like an automaton she obeyed, and sat, head drooping, as though her slender neck was too delicate to hold the heavy coil of silvery blonde hair.

After a moment she looked up and through a mist of hopeless anger and despair focused on his dark, autocratic face. 'You helped Richard, *planned* all of it, just to get a hold over me one way or another.'

Lips drawing back a little over white teeth, Zan made no attempt to deny the charge.

'How can you be so *vile*, so unscrupulous?'

He lifted his shoulders in a slight shrug. 'I had hoped it would prove unnecessary to use strong-arm tactics, but as it is... I intend to have you in my bed even if I'm compelled to do it the hard way.'

Seeing her almond eyes widen in panic, he said curtly, 'No, I don't mean rape, or brutality of any kind. I won't try to force you, or hurry you. I'll wait until you're willing——'

'I won't *ever* be willing,' she broke in raggedly.

In no way disconcerted, he said quietly, 'You seem very sure, but we'll see, shall we...?'

For one mad moment she was tempted to floor him by telling him *why* she was so sure. Then common sense prevailed. He had a knife at Richard's throat and, once he knew he would *never* achieve his ends, he might easily use it.

'In the meantime your brother will be safe so long as you do what I want you to do.'

Taking a deep breath she asked, 'What *do* you want me to do?'

'I want you to marry me. Be my wife.'

Feeling as though a giant fist was clenched round her heart, she choked, 'I'd rather be dead!'

He smiled bleakly. 'I doubt it. In any case, your being dead would hardly help Richard.'

It was the truth.

Her face half averted, her mouth desert dry, she swallowed convulsively, 'If I agreed, you wouldn't expect me to sleep with you?'

'I'm not asking for a full commitment at this stage, Annis, just a proper chance to get to know one another. I won't exert any undue pressure so long as you fulfil certain conditions.'

'What are the "conditions"?'

Calmly, he said, 'That there will be no other man in your life, and that apart from actually sleeping with me this marriage will, to all intents and purposes, be a real one.'

The first stipulation would be easy, the second wouldn't bear thinking about. 'For how long?'

He looked at her pure profile, the clean jawline, the small, neat nose, the thick fan of lashes, and appeared to consider. 'Shall we say a year?'

'A year!' Her head snapped round. 'You want to keep me a prisoner for a year!'

'There's really no call to be so melodramatic.' His voice was caustic.

Distraught, catching at straws, she cried, 'What about my business?'

'Miss Collingford appears to be running Help quite satisfactorily.'

'But I must have *something* to do...'

'If you want to go on working, you can work for me.'

'And there's my flat...'

After a moment, he said, 'Keep it on if you wish.'

Then with a glance at his watch, he rose to his feet, graceful as any big cat. 'Now I've some business to attend to that will take the rest of the afternoon. While I'm gone I suggest you think things over. If you decide to accept my terms, I'll expect to find you've moved your belongings in here and are waiting for me when I get back.' Casually, he added, 'Don't forget to bring your passport.'

Despite the *if*, he was quite obviously sure of her, *confident* she'd do as he wanted.

Slipping on his jacket, he fished in the pocket and dropped a black ornate key into her lap. 'I should be home about seven.'

He left without kissing her.

She told herself how pleased and relieved she was. Yet somehow the deliberate omission unsettled her and added to her consternation.

Think things over, he'd said, but what would thinking achieve? She could thrash about until she was exhausted but, like a cat tied in a sack, there was no escape, as well he knew.

If she refused to marry him, Zan was ruthless enough to bring all Linda's and Richard's new-found security tumbling around their ears, and she couldn't, *wouldn't* let that happen.

Yet his conditions were unacceptable.

To be in close proximity *for a year* to a man she loathed... To live in his house, be under constant threat and pressure...

But he could have demanded her *immediate* surrender.

It was a sobering thought.

As it was he'd been astute enough to offer terms which, though repugnant, seemed to hold out a fighting chance of her emerging relatively unharmed.

A sophisticated, experienced man, he must have been aware of the reluctant fascination she'd felt from the start. Clearly he was banking on that fascination growing and eventually luring her into his arms.

What he didn't know, so couldn't possibly have taken into account, was that she had such cause to hate him.

If she agreed to his conditions...

If? Her thoughts having come full circle, she admitted there was no *if* about it. They both knew she had no option and that was why, instead of crowding her, Zan had walked away, ostensibly leaving her free to make her own decision.

Becoming aware that the sharp metal edges of the key she'd automatically picked up were cutting painfully into her palm, she reached for her bag and dropped it in, before jumping to her feet with sudden determination.

At the same instant she heard a horn tooting insistently outside.

At the top of the drive a taxi was waiting.

She should have been expecting it. Zan thought of everything.

Rolling down his window, the driver asked, 'Where to, lady?'

Annis gave him her address and climbed in.

When they drew to a halt outside Fairfield Court, displaying a recklessness quite foreign to her nature, she asked the driver to wait.

She had relatively few clothes and personal possessions. Within twenty minutes everything she needed to take was packed, the bed had been stripped, the fridge cleared, and the few remaining provisions popped into a carton to give to her neighbour along with the laundry bag.

Pulling on her mac, she closed the door behind her with a strange feeling of finality.

When Mrs Neilson answered her knock, deciding to make her explanation as brief and unrevealing as possible, Annis said, 'I'm forced to be away for a while... It's very short notice, I know, but will you have a key and keep an eye on the place for me? Oh, and if any mail comes can you send it on to my office?'

'Of course I will, my dear. I'll be happy to pop round and do whatever's necessary.'

'Thanks,' Annis said gratefully. 'I'll stay in touch.'

'Don't be gone too long,' Mrs Neilson called. 'I'll miss you.'

Annis felt her eyes fill with tears. She hadn't thought anyone would like her enough to miss her.

After tragedy had struck, feeling to blame for having been unable to avert it, and sickened by all the avid curiosity and what she'd seen as spurious sympathy, she'd withdrawn into her shell.

Deliberately isolating herself, she'd avoided friends and acquaintances and eschewed contact with anyone, except on a superficial level.

Having tossed her suitcases into the boot, a look of speculation on his seamy face, the taxi driver asked, 'Back to Park Lane?'

'Yes, please,' she said coolly, and settled into her seat.

When they arrived at their destination and she reached for her bag to pay him, he shook his grizzled head. 'Mr Power's already taken care of it.'

And with his usual generosity, no doubt, Annis reflected wryly, as she thanked the man for carrying in her cases, and closed the door behind him.

Having hung her mac on the hall-stand, she left her luggage where it was and braced herself to look around.

One quick glance was enough to tell her that the housekeeper's quarters, which she didn't venture into, ran along the foot of the L.

Bearing in mind that the house belonged to a wealthy bachelor, she half expected to find it displayed the impersonal expertise of some expensive interior designer. But its panelled sitting-room, dining-room and study were simply furnished with what she guessed were individually chosen pieces. A miscellany which somehow came together to form a charming and harmonious whole.

Ascending the handsome staircase, she found there were five bedrooms, each with an en-suite bathroom.

The one which ran along the front of the house was obviously Zan's. Standing just inside the door, feeling like an intruder, she looked around her.

If she had subconsciously anticipated silken sheets and mirrored ceilings, the retreat of a sensualist, she couldn't have been more wrong.

The furniture was dark oak, and with plain white walls and ivory paintwork, an indigo carpet and matching curtains, the room was almost austere in its cool, elegant simplicity.

It struck her that it was a strange choice for a boy from the heat and confusion, the colourful earthiness of the slums of Piraeus.

Then she saw the picture opposite the bed. It was a portrait in oils of a Spanish dancer, vivid and sensuous, wearing a dress like flame.

The contrast was startling. Fire and ice.

Still feeling the after-effects of her bout of flu, she lugged her cases up the stairs one at a time and put them in the guest room furthest away from the master bedroom.

When she'd finished unpacking she made her way down to the cosy kitchen and, her nerves already starting to tighten at the thought of Zan's return, began to prepare an evening meal. By the time it was done a misty dusk had crept up to press against the window panes like damp grey fur, and the room was growing shadowy.

In a little over an hour he would be home.

She touched the main light switch and just for a split-second the kitchen was lit up. Then there was a sharp crack as the bulb blew and plunged it back into gloom.

Strip-lighting had been fitted above the various work-surfaces, and there were several lamps scattered about, but, finding the dim light oddly soothing, she refrained from putting any of them on.

Curled up in one of the deep armchairs, she watched the leaping flames, and waited for him to come home like someone awaiting the hangman.

CHAPTER FOUR

A SLIGHT sound disturbed Annis, and she opened heavy eyes to find in the semi-darkness a tall figure looking down at her.

Zan was standing absolutely still, as though transfixed.

One of the logs settled and flared, sending up a shower of bright sparks. As the red glow briefly illuminated his face she saw that he was staring at her with a passionate intensity.

He looked like a man who, on the steps of the guillotine, had suddenly, miraculously been reprieved.

His expression, and the realisation of what it meant, made her catch her breath.

Coming home to a dark and apparently empty house had shaken him badly, made him think she'd refused his terms—until he'd walked into the kitchen and discovered her there.

A shiver ran through her. One thing was frighteningly clear. Having her here was not just a passionate whim. It *mattered* to him.

That knowledge—the thought came sharp and clear as a laser beam—might give her a weapon to turn against him, a means of revenge.

But until she'd had a chance to think how best to use her accidental discovery of how strong his feelings were, she ought to play it cool. Make no reference to coercion, simply act as though she was a guest in his house.

If a reluctant one.

'Quite a good trick to play.' His voice was the slightest fraction uneven. 'You did it with malice aforethought, I presume?'

'Did what?'

'You know perfectly well what I mean.'

After a moment, she admitted, 'Yes, I do... And no, I didn't.'

'Then why were you sitting so quietly in the dark?'

'The bulb blew when I put the light on... I sat down to watch the fire, and I must have fallen asleep... What time is it?'

'Nearly seven o'clock.'

As he reached to switch on the nearest lamp, she struggled to her feet. 'I hope the casserole hasn't dried up.'

Discarding his jacket, he said curtly, 'I don't expect you to do the housekeeper's work.'

'I wasn't planning to,' she said mildly.

While he replaced the bulb, she warmed plates and took the food out of the oven.

For a while they ate in silence, then suddenly, surprising her, he said, 'I'm sorry. I'm not usually bad-tempered.'

What surprised her even more was that she believed him. Hard, relentless, tyrannical, ruthless...the adjectives she could apply to him were many, but ill-tempered wasn't one of them.

After a moment, when she said nothing, he admitted wryly, 'I hardly expected you to believe me.'

'But I do. You haven't the look of a bad-tempered man.'

His firm mouth twisted into a mocking smile. 'Do you know that's the first time you've ever said anything nice to me?'

'It may well be the last.'

'Pity. I was hoping we could live together in amity if not perfect harmony.'

'It seems unlikely, given the circumstances.' Remembering her earlier decision to play it cool, she regretted the pointed words as soon as they were spoken, and was pleased when he elected to ignore them.

The meal over, Zan waited courteously until Annis rose, then followed her to the fireside. Before she knew what he was about, he had lifted her left hand and slipped a magnificent diamond solitaire on to her third finger.

It was an excellent fit.

When she would have taken it off, he stopped her by the simple expedient of holding both her hands. 'You might as well keep it on.'

Trying to pull free, she cried, 'No, I don't want a ring. I won't wear it.'

Softly, adamantly, he overruled her. 'You'll wear it to please me, and to add veracity to our engagement.'

Taking her face between his palms, he studied the helpless rage in her eyes with a gleam in his own. 'I think a kiss to seal our bargain?' The dark, decisive voice was gently mocking.

When his mouth covered hers it was anything but gentle. His kiss, made up of fire and honey, of passion and dangerous excitement, left her shaking in his arms.

Opening dazed eyes, she stared up at him. He was smiling a little. Everything about him was hard and handsome, the strong nose and slanting cheekbones, the chiselled mouth and white teeth, the cleft in his firm chin. It was the face of a hunter, watchful and predatory.

'I hate you!' she whispered.

'Because I kissed you?'

'I didn't want you to.'

'Didn't you?' He looked vital and taunting. 'Are you quite sure?'

She *had* to be sure. It would be a tragedy to want him. Yet his magnetism was so powerful that it drew her in spite of all her hatred.

Bending his head, he kissed her again with a pagan sensuality, making the blood race frantically through her veins.

His tongue, balked by the barrier of her pearly teeth, stroked across the softness of her inner lip, bringing an anguished protest. '*Don't*.' She was desperate to move away from him, but her limbs had lost their power.

He stared down at her with gleaming eyes, his breathing a shade quick and erratic.

'Leave me alone,' she managed hoarsely, and from somewhere found sufficient strength to struggle. 'I don't want you to touch me.'

After a moment he sighed and, letting her go, said wryly, 'Then this might be a good time to visit Helen and Matt.'

Feeling drained, shattered, she was in no mood for visiting, but *anything* was better than being here alone with him, Annis thought shakily as she preceded him across the hall.

In a relatively short time they were drawing up outside the porticoed entrance of number fifteen Elwood Place.

Helen herself answered the door, and exclaimed, 'How nice to see you both. Come on in.'

As they followed her into a pleasant living-room, a man with smooth dark hair looked up and, seeing Annis, rose courteously to his feet.

He was tall and slimly built, a strikingly good-looking man, with fine, almost delicate features, and deep-set hazel eyes. If there was a touch of carnality to his mouth, a hint of self-indulgence in that handsome face, it only seemed to add to his attraction.

She recalled Stephen denying that Zan had a reputation as a Don Juan and adding, 'Matt Gilvary does, or rather *did*, before he became Mr Power's brother-in-law'... Yes, she could believe it, she thought now.

'Annis, this is my husband, Matt,' Helen said proudly.

'How do you do?' Annis smiled politely, and, meeting Matt Gilvary's eyes, found a warm, masculine appreciation in his glance.

'Do sit down,' Helen invited.

Zan shook his head. 'This is only a flying visit. We just came to tell you our news.' Putting a proprietorial arm round Annis's waist, he lifted her left hand and displayed the ring. 'Annis has agreed to marry me.'

A moment later Helen was hugging and kissing them both, crying, 'How marvellous! I'm so pleased.'

'Congratulations!' Matt clapped Zan on the shoulder.

The same general description of tall, dark, and handsome would have fitted them both, but as they stood together, Annis saw that the difference between them was striking. Zan, though equally lean, was better muscled and tougher-looking, with a more mature width of shoulder, and on power and attraction and pure animal magnetism he won hands down.

Matt, despite being as tall, and easily the better-looking of the two, seemed to fade into relative insignificance beside the other man.

When the pair had shaken hands, Matt asked, 'May I kiss my future sister-in-law?'

'So long as you don't turn her head,' Zan answered.

Grinning, Matt observed, 'She doesn't look like a woman whose head is easily turned. And in any case my wife is watching.'

Approaching Annis, who was standing like someone in a dream, he kissed her lightly on both cheeks.

'Welcome to the family. I hope you'll be able to keep him in order and——'

'Let us know when the wedding's going to be,' Helen broke in.

Matt groaned. 'You know what this will mean . . . a new outfit and an outrageously expensive hat . . .'

Smiling, Zan said, 'Make it a matron of honour's dress . . . And get moving. We're being married in four days' time by special licence.'

Annis felt as though she'd been pushed from a plane at thirty thousand feet without a parachute. She had hoped for some breathing space; she hadn't expected it to be *this* soon.

Amid exclamations of surprise and excitement, they were escorted across the hall.

At the door the two men exchanged a few words in an undertone before Zan settled Annis in the car and turned to wave.

During the short journey home he whistled softly, melodiously, while, pale and tense, staring straight ahead, Annis tried to still the butterflies fluttering in her stomach.

It was incredible to think that only that morning she'd awakened in her own bed feeling relatively cheerful, without a notion of how the day would end.

When they got back, she went straight through to the kitchen while Zan garaged the car. The clock on the mantelpiece showed it was still barely nine-thirty, but she felt bone-weary.

She was sitting staring blindly into the fire, wondering how on earth she was going to cope, when Zan strolled in and remarked, 'We ought to let your brother and sister-in-law know.'

Reaching for the phone, he dialled the number of the nursing home. Then, sitting on the arm of her chair, so close he brought her out in gooseflesh, he passed her the receiver.

After a couple of rings she heard Linda's clear voice answer, 'Hello?'

Her mind whirling with conflicting thoughts, she stammered, 'I-it's Annis...'

'Hi!' Linda sounded on top of the world. 'Just after you'd left this morning the doctor came round. He told me if I keep improving at this rate I should be out of here in a couple of days. *Home*. Isn't that wonderful?'

'It certainly is,' Annis agreed.

'I can hardly believe things have turned out so *marvellously*... Just imagine, if Mr Power hadn't——'

As though he'd been waiting for his cue, Zan took the phone from Annis's nerveless grasp and said, 'Make it Zan. In the circumstances we can dispense with formality... Annis and I are going to be married.'

'Married!' Linda's excited squeal could easily be heard. 'Our congratulations to you both. Have you a date fixed yet?'

Zan told her, adding, 'We'd like you to be a matron of honour, even if you have to follow the bride with your arm in a sling.'

Linda said something Annis didn't catch.

Laughing, he answered, 'Sorry... Neither of us wanted to wait... Yes, you could say that. We'll be in touch about the arrangements. Take care of yourself.'

Replacing the receiver, he remarked with some satisfaction, 'Your sister-in-law sounded pleased, and not unduly surprised...'

Of course he'd planned ahead, laid the ground well, Annis conceded bitterly. And she'd gone where he'd led, like a lamb to the slaughter.

'It appears she's a great believer in love at first sight.' Watching Annis's expressive face, he queried sardonically, 'Or were you intending to tell them the truth?'

'No, I wasn't,' she said baldly. There was no way she could do that. It would put a terrible burden of undeserved guilt on their shoulders...

Noticing the effort she was having to make not to droop, he said, 'You look all-in. I suggest an early night.'

There was a taut stillness, the air all at once filled with sexual tension.

He sighed. 'So now you're going to panic?'

'I don't need to, do I?' She strove to speak coolly. 'You did agree to separate rooms?'

'Of course.' He gave her a glinting look. 'Until you change your mind and *want* to move in with me.'

Dismissing the possibility, she said with cool disdain, '*If* that happens I'll tell you.'

'*When* it happens you won't need to tell me, I'll know.'

His absolute certainty made her break out in a cold perspiration. She wanted to scoff, to call such confidence overweening. But in a very short time, clearing all known obstacles from his path with ferocious speed, he'd got her practically where he wanted her.

Not only had she accepted his terms and his ring but in just four days they would be man and wife.

So hadn't he every reason to be confident?

It was a terrifying thought.

Determined not to let him see her consternation, head high, back ramrod-straight, she preceded him up the stairs.

At her bedroom door, when she would have gone straight in, he lightly took her arm, turning her towards him. Softly, he said, 'Goodnight, Annis. Sleep well.' A finger beneath her chin, he tilted her face up to his.

This time his kiss was light, in no way threatening. Different emotions chasing through her, she forced herself to stand quietly, without making any effort to pull away.

Hands spanning her slim waist, he suddenly turned on the heat, the tip of his tongue running across her lips in an erotic, exploratory caress.

Fire crackled along her nerve-ends and she gasped, her lips parting helplessly beneath the sweet, drugging demand of his.

As his tongue teased and tormented, head reeling, she swayed towards him, her palms flattening themselves against his chest. Through the thin sweater she could feel the solid bone and muscle, the heat of his flesh.

A torrent of passion ran through her, swift and molten. She was filled with a burning desire and her arms went around his neck and she clung to him, drowning in the scent of him, delighting in the contact with his lean, strong body.

Stop! Stop! Suddenly sanity screamed a warning, and horror at what was happening took the place of excitement.

Although the heated blood still rushed through her veins, her brain all at once became clear and icy-cool. If he was feeling the kind of hunger she was feeling, leading him on until he was fully aroused and then calling a halt was one way she could hurt him. Get revenge in some small degree.

He'd promised not to force her and, whatever his faults, she believed he'd keep his word.

But it was still a dangerous game to play, the voice of common sense warned her. Despite her hatred of him, *she* wasn't immune to *his* powerful sexual attraction. Though she would be if she kept remembering Maya, she told herself grimly.

Feeling her stillness, he drew back a little and looked down at her.

In that instant she knew that if she pulled away he would let her go.

Emboldened, she sighed and ran her fingers into his black hair, marvelling how the shorn curls, which looked so crisp, felt like silk.

He made a sound, half sigh, half groan, and his arms closed tightly around her, pulling her slender, fragile body to his.

'You're so lovely,' he muttered, 'and I want you to distraction...'

His kisses on her upturned mouth were sweeter than wine and just as heady. But she *had* to keep control.

Thickly, he admitted, 'I've wanted to hold you like this for what seems an age... I've even dreamt of making love to you...'

Now! Now! she told herself, and, summoning all her resolve, pulled away.

His dark face looked absorbed, almost dazed.

'You promised you wouldn't rush me,' she said accusingly, and held her breath.

She heard his teeth snap together. After perhaps five seconds, he admitted, 'So I did,' and turning on his heel, walked away.

With a sense of triumph she went into her own room and closed the door. Yes, she could do it! she told herself exultantly.

He was forcing her to marry him, but when they *were* married, instead of succumbing to his attraction, as he hoped, she would lead him on until he was almost frantic with passion and need, then spurn him as he'd spurned Maya.

The stronger, more urgent his desire for her, the better; the hurt would go deeper. And whilever he kept trying to make love to her, she would keep repeating that rejection.

The following Wednesday, at four o'clock on a cool but sunny afternoon, they were married by special licence in the Church of St George, Mayfair.

It had been decided that Annis should be married from Rydal Lodge, and earlier that day Zan had driven her over.

Apart from the actual wedding-party, only Zan's housekeeper—a sturdy, grizzled Scotswoman whose air of dourness was belied by a gleam of humour in the granite-grey eyes—was present at the ceremony.

Everyone appeared somewhat stunned by the speed at which events had moved.

Matt, good-looking and immaculate in morning dress, was Zan's best man, while Richard, equally prepossessing, gave the bride away.

Helen and Linda, clad in pale apricot silk, and excited as a pair of schoolgirls, made beautiful matrons of honour.

If the bride—tall and slender, ethereal in an ankle-length dress of ivory lace and georgette—seemed quiet and pale, and her darkly handsome groom looked stern and formidable, it was put down to the solemnity of the occasion.

Owing to the extremely short notice, Zan's other sister and brothers—scattered around the globe—were unable to be present, but all had sent their warmest good wishes.

After the ceremony Matt produced a camera and insisted on taking a whole series of photographs, before they went on to the Eden Park's wedding-reception suite for a champagne meal.

When they reached the hotel, throwing off his air of gravity, Zan became his smiling, urbane self and, for everyone's sake, Annis did her best to follow his lead.

The others hit it off well, finding plenty to talk about, while Helen's high spirits and Mary Matheson's dry humour added a sparkle to the proceedings.

It was Linda, looking happy and animated despite her sling, who remarked, 'You haven't mentioned a honeymoon. Are you going away?'

'Of course,' Zan said smoothly. 'But not until to-morrow morning.' He glanced at Annis, and with a glint in his eye added, 'I didn't fancy spending my wedding-night on an aircraft with three hundred other passengers.'

As Annis felt her cheeks start to burn, Helen asked, 'Where are you going? Or is it a secret?'

A barely perceptible glance passed between Zan and Matt, then blandly, Zan told her, 'It's a secret. Not even Annis knows...'

When the party finally broke up, the housekeeper—a self-confessed member of the 'early to bed, early to rise' brigade—was having difficulty smothering her yawns, and as soon as they arrived home she bade the newlyweds goodnight and retired to her quarters.

'Would you like a drink or anything before we go up?' Zan asked.

Annis shook her head. She felt exhausted and, now the necessity to appear happy in front of Linda and Richard was over, totally dejected, her spirits flat as a dead battery.

Over the past four days Zan had neither kissed nor touched her, and apart from discussing the wedding arrangements had scarcely spoken to her.

She should have been relieved, but somehow she wasn't. Like the lull before a storm, the ominous calm, the sense of *waiting*, had only served to add to her uneasiness.

Even Mrs Matheson had remarked on his taciturnity and, rightly guessing the cause, had said, 'Well, I'll no' be sorry when the wedding's over. I canna abide to see a grown man acting like some bairn with its nose pressed against a sweet shop window.'

Preceding him up the stairs now, still in her wedding finery, Annis recalled how she had held her breath and waited for the explosion. But, apparently used to his housekeeper's acid-tongued frankness, he'd just smiled grimly and let it go.

When she reached the room she'd been using, Zan's comment about his wedding-night sticking in her mind like a burr, Annis shot straight inside and, closing the door, turned the key in the lock.

Then, her breath coming fast, her heart thudding like a trip-hammer against her ribs, she stood with her back to the panels and waited for his reaction.

For a moment or two there was dead silence, then she heard his light, even footsteps carry on down the landing to his own room.

Relaxing, she heaved a sigh of relief, and turned to get her night things.

It came as an unpleasant shock to find that—presumably after she'd left for Rydal Lodge—all her clothes and belongings had been moved—no doubt into Zan's room.

Oh, well, she'd just have to manage.

Having taken off her shoes and stockings, she removed the simple lace coronet that she had pinned into place, and let her waist-length hair tumble down her back.

When she reached to undo her wedding-dress, however, she encountered a problem. It had a long, close-fitting bodice which was fastened right down the length of her spine with tiny covered buttons and loops. Even using a small button-hook provided by the shop, it had taken Helen quite a long time to do them all up.

After struggling—hampered by her hair—for what seemed an age, Annis was forced to acknowledge that though she'd managed to unfasten quite a few, there was no way she was going to get the rest undone without help.

Having weighed up the options, she balked at the thought of disturbing Mrs Matheson. She would sooner sleep in the dress...

But already its boned bodice was uncomfortably tight, and in the morning she would *still* have to ask for help.

Dreading the derision such an appeal would undoubtedly give rise to, in desperation she tried to tear the buttons free.

The attempt proved unsuccessful, and, hot and agitated, fighting back tears of anger and frustration, she was forced to admit defeat.

After waiting a moment or two to regain some degree of composure, she took the only option open to her. Head high, she walked barefoot along the landing and tapped at Zan's door.

There was no answer.

He wouldn't be asleep already, so he must be in the bathroom, or taking a shower.

Turning the handle quietly, she opened the door and peeped in. The lamp on the chest of drawers was still burning, casting a pool of bright light which left the rest of the room in shadow.

Leaving the door ajar, she slipped inside, mentally rehearsing how she would handle it. A casual 'I can't quite reach the middle ones...' Or, 'Can you just undo these...?' then she could retreat with her dignity intact.

'I wondered how long you'd be.' His soft remark made her almost jump out of her skin.

He was in bed, hands clasped behind his black, curly head, leaning back indolently against the pillows.

Waiting for her.

As the thought crossed her mind, he got up with that cat-supple agility she had come to know so well and, padding over to the door, shut and locked it with a flourish.

He was stark naked. Broad shouldered and lean-hipped, muscles rippling beneath skin like oiled silk, he looked a magnificent male animal.

Her throat closing up tight, she croaked, 'What are you doing?'

Calmly, he replied, 'Locking the door. And before you object, may I remind you that *you* set the precedent?'

There was such leashed passion, such sensuality and grace in the lines of his virile body, that a combination of excitement and fear tied her stomach in knots.

'Well, you can just unlock it.' She managed to sound a great deal more confident than she felt. 'I only came to ask you to——'

'Help you out of your dress? I'd be delighted to.' His voice, with that fascinating hint of foreign origin slightly more pronounced, was a purr. Smiling tigerishly, he advanced on her.

'Don't come any nearer,' she said sharply, backing away despite herself.

He stopped in his tracks and pointed out, 'I can hardly undo buttons from this distance.'

Hair slightly rumpled, tawny eyes gleaming, he looked so devastatingly, *hatefully* attractive that he took her breath away.

Distrusting the satisfaction in his eyes, the barely hidden triumph, she wished fervently that she hadn't come.

'Just don't get any ideas,' she warned. 'I've no intention of sleeping with you.'

'It's quite usual for the bride and groom to sleep together on their wedding-night.' He spoke soothingly, as though to some dim-witted child.

As she ground her teeth, he went on, 'In fact most people don't consider they're really man and wife until the marriage has been consummated.'

Her voice sounding hoarse, she said, 'You forced me to marry you, but you can't make me sleep with you.'

His expression hardened, and glimpsing the icy determination behind his mocking smile, she faltered, 'You won't...?'

'No, I won't. As I told you when we made our bargain, force of that kind has never been on the agenda. Now, about those buttons.'

Suddenly he was close. Much too close. Overpowering in his sheer maleness. Confident, maybe, that he didn't *need* force.

She retreated a step, saying agitatedly, 'I wish you'd put something on.'

Lifting a dark brow, he pointed out, 'I *am* your husband. And surely you've seen naked men before?'

Not in the flesh. Not this close. And never with the kind of physical beauty that sent her temperature soaring and made her whole body zing into life...

'But if it bothers you...' He reached for a short navy-silk robe and, pulling it on, tied the belt loosely, before suggesting, 'Suppose you turn around.'

She turned obediently, gathering her long silky hair and pulling it forward over one shoulder.

With a sure, light touch he dealt unhurriedly with the recalcitrant buttons. Inevitably his fingers brushed her skin, and she quivered.

The last one undone, he eased the dress from her shoulders and arms and, as it slipped to the floor, touched his lips to the nape of her neck while his hands came up to cup her breasts.

With a muffled protest she tried to move away, but the froth of material around her ankles made walking impossible.

He drew her back against the warmth of his body, imprisoning her there. Before she could regain either her wits or her balance, his mouth was travelling up the side of her neck and across the soft skin beneath her chin, making her shiver with pleasure.

Turning her into his arms, he made a small sound at the back of his throat, almost like a groan, and kissed her with a sweet hunger, and overwhelming desire.

The voice of sanity was urging her to break free, when she recalled her vow to be revenged. Instead of pulling away she would pretend to surrender, make him think she was his for the taking. Then, when he was fully aroused, almost out of his mind with passion and need, she would reject him.

It would be easy so long as she retained her self-control.

Deliberately she pressed herself against him, and a shock-wave ran through her at the feel of his hard, muscular body. They fitted together as though made for each other, two separate parts making one complete whole.

His lips began to move over her face, planting soft baby kisses, before returning to hers to coax them apart and, like some alchemist, turn the steel of her self-control into molten gold.

Within a heartbeat she was a captive, caught and held by an invisible web of allure. In spite of her hatred he beguiled her so, fascinated and enchanted her.

By the time the rest of her delicate lingerie had followed the dress floorwards, she was utterly lost, her body burning with the longing his roving hands were igniting. And when he lifted her high in his arms and carried her to the bed, her arms wound round his neck and her lips clung to his.

He stretched out beside her and put his mouth to her breast. Hardly able to bear the exquisite torture, she gasped and jerked.

'Easy, darling,' he whispered. 'It's all right. It's all right... We'll take it slowly... But I want you to discover the explosive potential you've so resolutely locked away. I want to capture your imagination, fill your heart and mind, entice you into my arms and bewitch you so you never want to leave them...'

The dark sorcery of his words held her spellbound while he continued to seduce and ravish her senses.

She was nothing but a seething mass of sensations, her whole body waiting, yearning for his, when he whispered, 'Look at me, Annis.'

Opening her eyes, she looked dazedly up into his dark face.

His voice husky, uneven, he said, 'I have to know. *Was* Stephen your lover?'

The urgent query shattered the spell of enchantment like a stone from a catapult shattering a fragile glass sphere.

Shocked and shivering, knowing how close she'd come to disaster, she played for time while she tried to collect herself. 'What do you think?'

Pinning her there with his look, he said, 'Damn you, don't tease me. *Was he*?'

She should be glad she'd regained her senses, not feel this wrenching sadness, this aching sense of loss. 'Does it matter?'

'Yes, it matters,' he told her passionately. 'I want to be the one to awaken you to the delights of love. I want to be the first to teach you about pleasure, so pure and delicate and satisfying, so exquisite that it's almost pain...'

Wriggling free of him, she sat up, her arms crossed protectively over her breasts, and forced herself to remark mockingly, 'I had no idea virgins were your cup of tea. I would have thought experienced women were more to your taste.'

A shade roughly, he said, 'In the past any relationship has been light, unimportant, involving nothing but an easy exchange of pleasure. Experienced women who know the score don't get hurt...'

Experienced women who know the score don't get hurt...

'You're the only woman who's ever mattered. The only woman I've ever felt this way about. I want to be your first lover. Your only lover...'

But Maya had got hurt, and she wanted him to suffer for it, to be almost out of his mind, trapped in a permanent state of frustration, his libido playing havoc with his self-control.

'Sorry,' she said with deliberate contempt, 'but I've gone off the idea. Some other time, maybe.'

Tawny eyes blazing, he seized hold of her upper arms, his fingers sinking into the soft flesh. 'Why, you little...' Seeing every vestige of colour drain from her face, he bit off the angry words.

Her heart in her mouth, she watched him fight for control, and win. Slowly his fingers loosened their grip. His hands dropped to his sides. 'If you've "gone off the idea",' savagely he mimicked her words, 'you'd better go while I can still keep my promise.'

Striding over to the door, he unlocked it and held it open.

Without waiting to pick up her clothes, she fled.

Revenge was supposed to be sweet, but this time there was no triumph, no sense of elation, just desolation and a gnawing ache.

Huddled naked beneath the bedclothes, knees drawn up, eyes closed tightly, she lay awake for a long time shivering with a combination of nerves and misery before sleep claimed her.

Subconsciously dreading the morning, knowing she'd have to face Zan's anger, she slept badly, and woke feeling tired and headachy.

But to her surprise he seemed his normal self when, at seven o'clock, he brought her a cup of tea.

He studied her wan face, the dark shadows beneath her beautiful eyes, but, making no reference to the previous night, said merely, 'We shall need to be at the airport by mid-morning at the latest.'

New anxieties crowding in on her, she demanded, 'Where are we going? And for how long?'

'San Francisco, for a few days, then on to Hawaii for two or three weeks. We should get plenty of sunshine, but San Francisco can be breezy, so when you do your packing you'd better put in something warm and windproof.'

Given the circumstances the long flight to California could well have proved intolerable, but in the event it was made relatively easy by Zan's determinedly friendly and pleasant manner.

She found he was a stimulating and entertaining companion with a good—and hitherto unexpected—sense of humour.

Even more surprising was the discovery that they had a lot in common, enjoying the same kind of books and music, and sharing a love for the live theatre.

With the eight-hour time difference they came in to land at San Francisco International Airport in the early afternoon.

It was a bright sunny day with a stiff breeze making white horses on the blue waters of the Bay, and beyond the San Andreas Rift a beautiful view of the distant Montara mountain.

All the formalities completed, they took a cab and headed north into the city. The journey, following the US101 with its enticing glimpses of the Bay, was completed in silence, except for Zan pointing out landmarks and places of special note.

'If you're at all interested in baseball or American football,' he lifted a questioning brow, 'that's Candlestick Park, where the SF Giants and the SF Forty-niners battle it out.'

When they reached Union Square, with its smart boutiques, large department stores, and bright flower stands—the heart, so he told her, of the affluent downtown district—the taxi drew up in front of the luxurious Cliff Lobos Hotel.

Zan paid off the laconic, gum-chewing driver and, while a couple of bell-hops hurried to deal with the luggage, ushered her into the ultra-modern lobby, striking and spectacular with an indoor waterfall and hanging gardens.

The manager, slim and dapper, hurried out to greet them.

They took the lift up to the fourteenth floor and with due ceremony were shown around their elegantly furnished apartment, which comprised two bedrooms with en-suite bathrooms and a large central sitting-room with one wall made almost entirely of tinted glass.

Annis, standing looking out across the handsome square, had to resist the temptation to pinch herself. She felt oddly disorientated, as if she had been whisked up and deposited there by magic. So much had happened so quickly that events had almost outstripped her capacity to take in and register them.

In just two weeks he had taken over her life. From being strangers they were now man and wife.

On honeymoon.

Suddenly, unnervingly, she recalled how close she'd been to complete surrender the previous night.

In her mind she both hated and feared him, yet the female in her couldn't help but respond to his powerful sex appeal, his potent maleness.

She shivered.

Though getting through the coming days, not to mention the nights, would prove as hazardous as picking her way through a minefield, all she needed to do, she told herself firmly, was stay cool.

But how long could she stay cool if Zan chose to turn on what amounted to a sexual blowlamp?

CHAPTER FIVE

AFTER the manager and his entourage had departed, Zan strolled across to join her at the wide expanse of glass.

'Shattered?' he asked, studying the delicate purity of her profile.

'A bit,' she admitted coolly.

'That's not surprising. But I've found the best way to adjust to the time difference is to keep awake, if you can, until it's bedtime here.'

When she said nothing, he added, 'So, when you've had a chance to freshen up, I thought we might go out and take a closer look at the Bay.'

'It's up to you.'

He shook his head. 'No, it's up to *you*.'

Resisting the temptation to retort that if it was up to *her* she wouldn't be here with him at all, she said flatly, 'A look at the Bay sounds nice.'

'Say half an hour?'

When she nodded agreement, he disappeared into his own bedroom, closing the door behind him.

After unpacking and having a refreshing shower, she put on a fine wool grey and cream pleated skirt and a plain cream top. She had just selected a light, wind-proof, three-quarter-length coat when there was a tap on the door.

Making it plain that his knock was a mere courtesy, Zan walked in without waiting for permission.

He had changed from the well-cut suit he'd travelled in, and was casually dressed in pale trousers and a dark polo-necked sweater. A corduroy jacket was slung over his shoulder and held by one crooked finger.

His shorn black curls still damp from the shower, his green-gold eyes brilliant, showing no sign of tiredness, he looked fit as a fiddle and dangerously attractive.

'Ready?'

'Yes.' Her answer sounded oddly husky.

His slight but knowing smile made it clear he'd correctly interpreted the cause of her disturbance.

Soft mouth firming, head held high, she led the way out to the lift.

Deliberately, it seemed, he stood so close she could smell the freshness of his aftershave, feel the warmth of his body.

Somehow she resisted an intense urge to move further away, knowing only too well what he would make of such a reaction. But her heartbeat and breathing quickened, and her skin prickled with a sensual awareness.

It was only too easy to see how Maya had become infatuated with him, she thought bitterly. But how could *she* feel so strongly about a man she hated?

If only there were some way of cutting off that magnetism, exorcising the unwanted attraction. It put her in such danger...

Feeling trapped, desperately vulnerable, she fought down the apprehension and squared her shoulders resolutely. If she refused to let herself be rattled, somehow she would cope.

In spite of all her anxiety, entranced by its picturesque hills and blue water setting, its beautiful buildings and vibrant atmosphere, Annis fell in love with windy San Francisco that very first afternoon.

Over the next few days, rather to her surprise, Zan made no further attempt to turn on the heat and though always keenly *aware* of his presence, his every move, she started to feel less tense.

Only if he slid a casual arm around her, placed a friendly hand on her shoulder, or bent—his lips brushing her ear—to whisper to her, did she freeze and find it difficult to breathe, his lightest touch an intimacy that shook her.

As soon as he sensed that mental withdrawal, he invariably moved away, allowing her to breathe easily once more.

Bestowing only the one brief kiss—which she'd come to accept, almost *expect*—before heading for his own room each night, he seemed quite content to keep things on a light, comfortable footing.

At least for the present.

Greatly relieved by his determinedly platonic attitude, she found the following days were some of the most interesting and enjoyable of her life.

The weather was more than kind to them, conjuring up only blue skies, sunshine and good visibility, and none of the notorious coastal fogs that rolled in with such dramatic suddenness.

Sightseeing from morning until night, they rode on the old-fashioned clanging cable-cars, enjoyed a stroll along Fisherman's Wharf—with its fascinating street entertainers and wonderful views of the Bay—ate bowls of steaming seafood with their fingers, watched the sea lions at Pier Thirty-nine, and caught a ferry across to the island fortress of Alcatraz.

They walked over the elegant single-span of the Golden Gate Bridge—with its distinctive coat of international orange paint—visited Coit Tower and the Cannery, followed the Forty-nine-Mile Scenic Drive, and shopped at the exciting Ghirardelli Square complex.

Each day they talked, finding plenty to say to one another. And, without realising it, Annis had started to smile spontaneously again.

After several evenings spent dancing and dining, Zan suggested a visit to the Opera House to hear *Tristan and Isolde*.

Having booked the tickets, they returned to the hotel early to bathe and change before dinner.

In a lazy mood, Annis dawdled, and was still in her peach robe, her silvery-blonde hair loose, when with a perfunctory tap Zan walked in.

He looked sexily elegant, his long legs and lean hips encased in dark trousers, his white silk shirt still open at the neck to show his strong throat and the beginning of crisp body hair.

Unconsciously she licked her dry lips.

As he watched the betraying flick of her tongue, a flame ignited in his green-gold eyes. Intent on her mouth, he slowly bent his dark head.

Knowing she had to deflect him from his purpose, she jerked away and in a cracked voice demanded, 'What do you want?'

He smiled like a tiger.

Backing involuntarily, she said agitatedly, 'Why did you come in? If you hold me up, I won't be ready in time.'

'I came to ask if you would like an aperitif...' He advanced on her relentlessly. 'But now I'm going to have to kiss you, or I'll go mad.'

Trapped between him and the dressing-table, she was looking desperately for an escape route when his hand curled round her throat, lifting her face, and his mouth closed over hers. Panicked by the suddenness of the assault, she started to struggle.

As her body moved against his she heard him groan, and stilled, knowing her movements were only firing the conflagration she feared.

If he should lose control, he was so much stronger than she was, and the thin, silky robe offered little or no protection...

Feeling her absolute stillness, Zan lifted his head. '*Annis*...' His voice sounded anguished. 'What do you *do* to me?' He rested his forehead against hers. 'I don't know if I can take much more of this. I've never wanted a woman in my life the way I want you.'

'Then let me go,' she said swiftly. '*I* don't want *you*, so let me go.'

'You *do* want me,' he contradicted. 'You want me very much. But there are two people inside you, the self who responds to me and an alter ego I can't control.'

Sitting on a gilt-backed chair, he pulled her on to his knee.

'Don't...' There was fright in her cry.

'Sit still.' He brought up his hand, and with a curious tenderness brushed the pale silky hair back from her cheek. 'I want to talk to you...'

She sat stiff and silent in the circle of his arms, her heart banging against her ribs so hard she thought he must surely feel it.

After a moment he said gently, 'Somehow we didn't get off to a very good start, you and I. Your alter ego appeared to dislike and distrust me on sight, and I've had to force you every step of the way.

'Though you may find it hard to believe, as far as personal relationships go that's not my style. The women in my life have always been more than willing...'

She could believe *that*, Annis thought wildly, recalling Maya's besotted face, her husky voice crying, 'I'd do *anything* to be with him...'

'...but I was so terribly afraid of losing you.'

Amazed by the admission, her eyes flew to his face. Just for an instant his expression was unguarded. She read confusion there, a derisive self-contempt at his own vulnerability.

He hadn't mentioned the word 'love'. But his desire for her clearly went deeper than just wanting. Somehow she was *necessary* to him.

That being so, each rejection would wound him more seriously than merely scratching the surface of his male ego... Except that she was no longer sure of her own ability to lead him on and then walk away unscathed.

Holding her hand, his thumb stroking over the soft palm, he went on, 'A little while ago you asked me what I wanted...' He smiled a shade wryly, unused to begging. 'I want to wipe the slate clean and make a new start...'

The hard, ruthless, egotistical despot was gone. In his place was a man whose feelings ran deep, and who was capable of the most exquisite tenderness as well as passion. A softer, more human man, who was ready to allow he wasn't infallible; admit he was open to being hurt.

'I want you to want me, to come to me...'

Annis felt a deep and overwhelming attraction, on the brink of losing not only the struggle, but her heart as well.

Then, like a warning, she recalled the legend of the powerful Zeus who, finding that strength wouldn't gain him admittance to his quarry's house, turned himself into a baby and lay crying on the doorstep until he was carried inside.

Still she sat as though held in thrall, gazing into those fascinating green-gold eyes, his charm and magnetism making him totally irresistible.

She'd thought herself protected by her hatred of him, but as though that was suddenly irrelevant, she found herself caught and held in a magical spell of enchantment.

Deadly enchantment... As Maya had found to her cost.

Recoiling suddenly, she jumped up, and heart racing, cried, 'I don't want to make a new start... I'll *never* want you and I'll *never* come to you.'

Sloughing off the cloak of weakness, he got to his feet. Standing tall and supremely confident, he told her, 'Despite that coating of ice, the look of a Snow Queen, I don't believe any woman who has a mouth like yours can be frigid.

'You're young and healthy with natural feelings and needs. My terms stated no other man in your life so sooner or later those needs will betray you...'

Annis clenched her teeth, silently repudiating his words. Knowing how fierce emotional and physical needs, unchecked, unrestrained, had ruined Maya's life and finally destroyed her, *she* had learnt well how to control and repress them.

'Then you'll come to me willingly, wanting me as much as I want you.'

Oh, but she never would! For one mad moment she was tempted to tell him *why*. To throw the past in his face and watch his discomfort when he realised who she was.

Only she knew he wouldn't *feel* any discomfort. Any shame or guilt. As far as men like him were concerned, women were expendable. There to be used and discarded when they lost their appeal.

Lifting her head, she looked at him with icy disdain. 'You're quite wrong. If you were the only man left alive I wouldn't be willing.' Shuddering at the evocative brutality of the word, she said with finality, 'It would have to be rape.'

She saw the darkness behind those brilliant eyes, the unshakeable purpose.

'You won't...?' Her voice, unconsciously begging for reassurance, was scarcely above a whisper.

'Force won't be necessary.' He sounded so *sure*.

But recalling that anguished, 'I don't know if I can take much more of this,' for the second time she found herself doubting his self-control.

Reading her expressive face, he assured her mockingly, 'I can be patient if I must.'

She had a disturbing mental picture of a sleek black panther silently watching its prey. Waiting for that prey to weaken. Waiting to pounce.

Smiling a little crookedly, he added, 'It will be quite entertaining to see how long you can hold out.'

Heart thudding, she asked, 'What if your patience comes to an end and you get tired of waiting?'

'*If* that should happen I give you my word you'll be free to go without it affecting your brother in any way.'

It was as dangerous as living on the slopes of an active volcano, wondering when it might erupt and devastate her precarious existence. But if she could only hold out until he got totally frustrated and sick of waiting...

Of course she could hold out, she told herself hardily. Though she felt this strong and unwanted physical attraction, she *hated* him.

It was that hatred, combined with her repressions and inhibitions, which should protect her, keep her safe.

Should...

An alarm bell rang in her mind, warning how only a short time ago she'd come close to being enthralled by him.

But, having been rocked by that near disaster, there was no way she would let it happen again.

For Annis, *Tristan and Isolde* was a marvellous and moving experience, and she returned to the hotel in an ecstatic mood.

In the living-room a supper trolley was waiting, with a bottle of champagne on ice. Shaking her head at the sandwiches, Annis stood by the window sipping the cool, sparkling wine, while Wagner's wonderful love music continued to weave its spell in her mind.

In another world, she scarcely noticed when, more than once, Zan refilled her glass.

When he said his usual, 'See you in the morning. Sleep well...' relaxed, floating a little, she lifted a soft-eyed, dreamy face for his goodnight kiss.

It started as a light, almost casual touch, but when her lips parted beneath that slight pressure, he immediately deepened the kiss.

Almost at once coherent thought blurred into mindless sensation. His mouth moving against hers was the only thing in the universe that mattered.

Her arms went around his neck and she swayed against him, her fingers running into his hair, holding his head.

His hands began to rove over her slender curves with a kind of passionate tenderness that perfectly echoed what she was feeling.

If, at that stage, he'd shown any sign of hesitation, or rushed things, or spoken a single word, the mood might have been broken.

But as though it was the most natural thing in the world, in silence and with consummate skill he made love to her, his kisses and caresses bringing a singing delight that overwhelmed her.

She shuddered as he found her breasts, cupping and fondling them through the thin silk of her dress, his thumbs gently stroking the sensitive nipples so they sprang into erotic life.

Was it her heart or his that beat so loudly?

His voice hoarse, he whispered, 'I've waited for this moment...' and, strangely, those confident hands trembled.

When he carried her through to her room and undressed them both, she was lost, clinging to him blindly, mindlessly, wanting only the feel of his body against hers, the ultimate passion and tenderness of his possession.

The brief, tearing pain she felt at his first strong thrust only served to intensify the ecstasy until, like a phoenix, she burnt up gladly, joyfully, in the flames.

Long before the ashes had time to cool, held against Zan's heart she fell deeply asleep.

She awoke slowly, languorously, opening heavy lids to golden Californian sunshine. Her body warm with satisfaction and contentment, she stretched luxuriously and wriggled her toes.

But, while her senses revelled, her mind, as though still drugged, lay quiescent.

Only when Zan strolled into the room wearing a short white towelling robe and clearly fresh from the shower did it stir into horrified realisation of what she'd done.

Looking fit and virile, his handsome face alight with happiness, he was whistling quietly, melodiously, half under his breath.

Seeing she was awake, he came over to the bed and, smiling, his green-gold eyes brilliant, he stooped to kiss her. He was cool and fresh, smelling faintly of minty toothpaste and aftershave.

'You even wake up beautiful,' he observed. Adding softly, 'If there wasn't a need to get moving, I'd rejoin you. As it is, the cab I've hired to take us to the airport will be here shortly, and our brunch is already waiting.' He kissed her again, his mouth lingering on hers.

Neither responding nor resisting, she could have been an ivory statue. Every feeling and emotion seemed to have drained out of her.

When she continued to lie there without speaking or moving, his tone teasing, he said, 'Come on, then, lazy-bones... Or are you just feeling modest?'

Picking up her dressing-gown, he drew back the bedclothes.

Galvanised into action by the realisation that she was naked, she snatched at the gown and, pulling it on, fled to the bathroom.

While mechanically she cleaned her teeth and showered, the full import of what had taken place the previous night began to register in her dazed mind, and she groaned aloud.

She had told herself she was safeguarded by her hatred, and by the inhibitions caused through knowing how unrestrained passions could ruin her life. But neither hatred nor inhibitions had been strong enough to prevent her surrender.

Shudder after shudder running through her, she wanted desperately to deny the whole thing, to change what had happened, obliterate it. But it couldn't be denied, or changed, or obliterated. It was a fact.

In the first rush of bitterness she tried to blame Zan for everything. But an innate honesty insisted it was her own fault. She had lost her head completely.

Now she knew exactly how Maya had felt.

Wanting him, *loving* him, *she* was the one who had gone up in flames and started the unstoppable conflagration.

No! She rejected the thought violently. She *couldn't* love a man like Zan. Her mind must be unhinged even to suggest such a thing.

Yet, while indifference could stretch endless and empty as no man's land, it was said that love and hatred, such powerful emotions, had only a very thin dividing line.

The concept had become hackneyed, a cliché, yet, as most clichés did, it contained a terrible truth. And somehow, while she hadn't been looking, she had inadvertently stepped over that line.

Now she *had* to step back before she was utterly lost...

'Nearly ready to eat?'

Zan's tap on the door, his brisk query, made her jump and wake up to the fact that she was still standing in the shower bare and shivering, drops of cold water trickling down her long slim legs.

Finding her voice, she called, 'I'll be there in a minute,' and was surprised by how *normal* she sounded.

When she emerged a short time later, wrapped in a towelling robe, it was to find a young black maid doing her packing.

Clean undies and a matching cotton skirt and jacket had been laid out on the bed.

The girl looked up with a smile and, indicating the suit, remarked, 'Mr Power suggested you might like to travel in this, ma'am, but if you'd prefer something else?'

Making an effort to return the smile, Annis said, 'Oh, no, that will do fine, thanks.'

As soon as she'd dressed and coiled her silvery blonde hair into its usual elegant chignon, she braced herself and, hating the thought of having to face Zan, went through to the living-room.

Dressed in a lightweight suit, he was lounging in one of the deep armchairs while he flicked through a copy of the *San Francisco Herald*.

At her entrance he tossed the paper aside and rose to his feet with that supple cat-like movement she now knew well.

Showing the courtesy that seemed to come naturally to him, he settled her at the small trolley-table, before taking a seat opposite.

Careful not to meet his eyes, she helped herself to a flapjack she didn't want and spread maple syrup over it, while he poured fresh orange juice for them both.

She could sense a change in his attitude. From being happy, almost exultant, he was now quiet, no longer so sure of her, made cautious by her manner.

They ate in silence until the maid came in to say everything was packed and, at the same instant, the bell-hops arrived to deal with the baggage.

While Annis finished her coffee, Zan handed out tips with his usual generosity. A moment later the bustle of activity had ceased and they were alone.

Judging that he was ready to leave, still avoiding his eyes, she picked up her shoulder-bag and, more than eager to be gone, made for the door.

She had almost reached it when his fingers closed lightly yet purposefully round her arm, stopping her in her tracks.

His other hand cupping her chin, he tilted it, making her breath flutter in her throat and her heart stop, then start to beat again with slow, painful thuds.

Gazing down at her cool, aloof face, the small straight nose, the heavy fan of silk lashes almost brushing her high cheekbones, the lovely curve of her lips, he said quietly, 'You haven't once looked at me this morning, and I'd like to know why.'

Not knowing what to say, she tried to prevaricate. 'I thought you were in a hurry to get off.'

'Before we go anywhere I want to know what the matter is. Why you're treating me like some kind of leper.'

When she remained silent, he said quietly, 'Look at me, Annis.'

Reluctantly she obeyed, only her beautiful aquamarine eyes betraying her agitation.

His clean-cut mouth was grim and a slight frown drew his black brows together. 'I want an answer. I want to know what's wrong—*why* you're acting like this. Do you think that everything that happened last night was my fault?'

'No.' Her voice was full of anguish. 'I blame myself.'

'Why are you *blaming* yourself? We *are* married...' He sighed. 'Surely it can't be because of Stephen? I know now he'd never been your lover. You were as virginal as that Snow Queen image had suggested.'

Seeing the faint tinge of colour that stained her cheeks, he said urgently, 'Did you think that when it came to the point you *might* be frigid? Did it come as a shock to find you weren't?'

She shook her head.

'Then why are you giving yourself hell for behaving like a warm, passionate woman?'

When she didn't answer, he took her upper arms and shook her a little. 'I don't want you to have any regrets. It was wonderful. Natural and joyous. And I'm damned if I'll let you retreat behind those walls of ice again...'

A polite knock interrupted his words. With a muttered oath he released her, and opened the door to find the manager waiting to wish them a pleasant journey, and escort them down to their cab.

Annis began to move like a sleepwalker, the expression on her lovely face withdrawn, abstracted. Reaching for her hand, Zan tucked it through his arm and held it there with strong, lean fingers.

Afterwards she could recall little of their departure. Divorced from reality, blind and deaf to everything going on around her, Zan's words kept running through her mind... 'It was wonderful... Natural and joyous...' and, in spite of all her efforts to the contrary, she found herself reliving the previous night.

She recalled the potent, masculine scent of his smooth olive skin, the ripple of his chest muscles, the light sprinkling of crisp hair beneath her palms.

Felt again the exquisite torment of his mouth at her breast, the molten pleasure as her body joyfully accepted his, the spiralling delight, and the final heart-stopping rapture.

She heard his harsh gasp, a cry that was her name, and felt the weight of his black head on her breast...

But this time, instead of floating on a warm sea of ecstasy and tenderness, she was grounded on the sharp rocks of anger and bitterness and humiliation, and scourged herself for her stupidity in allowing it to happen.

How *could* she have let herself sleep with the man who was responsible for destroying almost everything she'd once held dear?

So great was her agitation that they had gone through the departure procedure and were ready to board the plane before she managed to find some degree of calm.

A hand at once masterful and solicitous at her waist, his dark head inclined towards her, Zan escorted her up the steps to the aircraft.

When they'd been welcomed aboard and shown to their seats, he took her hand and gave it a squeeze. 'I'm sure you'll like Hawaii.'

She snatched her hand away, then, becoming aware that the attentive stewardess was hovering, she wiped all traces of hostility from her tone and asked evenly, 'Which island are we going to?'

'Oahu.' A gleam in his eye, he added, 'I thought it would be appropriate. Americans call it the honeymoon island.'

Knowing he was baiting her, and wanting to hit back, she said with saccharine sweetness, 'I'm surprised you can spare the time for a honeymoon... a big successful man like you.'

Showing no sign of being rattled, he answered mildly, 'A "big successful man like me" learns how to pick the right people for key positions, how to delegate. And Matt will take care of anything out of the ordinary that crops up.'

When she said nothing, he continued blandly, 'I haven't had a break for some time, and I thought a honeymoon in the sun would do you good after your recent illness...'

She swallowed the bitterness rising like bile in her throat. If he imagined that having once slept with him she would happily continue to do so, he had a surprise coming, not to say a shock, when he discovered that the 'honeymoon' was already over.

Once again she struggled to keep her voice level as she queried, 'Where exactly are we staying?'

'Do you know Oahu at all? If you do, it will probably sound a contradiction in terms when I say a secluded little bay just outside Waikiki. It's called Lani Hameha.'

Disliking the word 'secluded', her voice had sharpened perceptibly as she admitted, 'I know very little about Oahu, or Hawaii as a whole, except that it's America's only tropical state. Though of course I've heard of Waikiki.'

'Then you'll be aware that it's the main tourist resort, and next door Honolulu is the state capital and America's most exotic city...'

Seeing she wasn't inclined towards conversation, he said nothing further, and for the remainder of the rather bumpy flight across the Pacific to Honolulu International Airport, they spoke very little.

When the airport formalities had been completed, proving Zan's efficiency yet again, a hired Cadillac was waiting for them.

It was still sunny, and appreciably warmer than it had been in San Francisco, with balmy trade winds replacing the fresh salty breeze.

By the time they reached Lani Bay the sun had set with all the dramatic suddenness of the tropics. In the deep blue dusk, Waikiki's two and a half miles of beach-fronted high-rise development glittered like some jewel-encrusted sash.

But the tiny bay, looking like a travel poster with its sweep of pale sand ringed by feathery palms and the volcanic bulk of Diamond Head black against the evening sky, was deserted.

Annis felt a shiver of apprehension run down her spine.

Instead of the quiet hotel she had been expecting, their destination proved to be a white frame-built house. The yellow light spilling from its windows cheered her somewhat.

It was a split-level construction built on a gentle slope down to the bay and almost hidden from the road by trees and tropical vegetation.

Zan drew the car to a halt on the paved area behind the top level. 'Lani House,' he told her, satisfaction in his tone.

'Is it yours?' Despite her unease, somehow she kept her voice steady.

He shook his head. 'It belongs to Helen and Matt. I arranged with Matt to borrow it.'

As he helped her from the car, the front door opened and a man and woman emerged. Both were dark-haired islanders, with broad Polynesian-type faces and beaming white smiles.

'Annis, this is Hiawa and Hattie Akaka,' Zan said.

'*Aloha.*' Hattie's voice was deep and warm. 'Welcome to Oahu.' Stepping forward, she hung a *lei* of flowers around both their necks. The pale, waxy blooms were fresh and cool and exquisitely perfumed.

Smiling back, Annis thanked the woman with genuine pleasure.

While Hiawa helped Zan to carry in the luggage, Hattie, friendly and garrulous, showed Annis around the small but seemingly spacious house.

The bedrooms were at road level, and from a central hall a flight of stairs led down to a well-equipped dining-kitchen, while the long, airy sitting-room, with its open-fronted veranda, looked over a terraced garden to the bay.

It was a quiet idyllic spot. But one that Annis would happily have exchanged for the frenetic bustle of Waikiki itself.

'There's a tray of drinks waiting on the veranda, and in case you're hungry I've left a supper of cold meat and salad...' Hattie was saying.

With a sinking heart, Annis asked, 'Then you and Hiawa don't live here?'

'Oh, no.' Hattie gave her wide smile and led the way back upstairs. 'We only keep an eye on the place for Mr and Mrs Gilvary. We live in a condominium at the Waikiki Sunrise. During the day Hiawa helps with the hotel's water sports, and I work at the beach café-bar...'

All too soon, Hiawa and Hattie had said their goodbyes and were ready to leave. Having thanked the cheerful pair for their services, she and Zan accompanied them to their dusty truck, which was parked beneath some straggly pine trees.

Standing in the velvet dusk, Zan's proprietorial arm around her waist, the scent of the cool *leis* in her nostrils, Annis watched them drive away with a feeling that was close to panic.

But she mustn't *let* herself panic. All she had to do was keep calm, and make it abundantly clear to Zan that last night—rather than being the surrender he wanted—had been an aberration on her part. Something she had no intention of repeating...

CHAPTER SIX

'WE'LL sit on the veranda, shall we? The view's wonderful at night.' Zan's voice, full of dark sorcery, broke into Annis's uneasy thoughts.

He led her beneath the resinous pines to where a flight of wooden steps with a bark-covered handrail meandered down to the shadowy garden.

Over her head leaves and branches made black silhouettes, while a huge, glowing moon hung just above the palms. Mingling with the sweet scent of flowers was the spicy smell of green ginger and a faint salt tang from the sea.

Gentle waves whispered on to the shore and, just beyond the garden, Annis could see the white surf embroidering lacy traceries along the sand.

From the lawn two steps led up to the wooden veranda, which had some comfortable-looking cane furniture and was lit by a string of small candle-lanterns. A tray, covered by a piece of spotless muslin weighted round the edges with coloured glass beads, was waiting on the table. When Zan had poured fresh fruit cocktails chinking with ice into two tall glasses, they went to lean on the polished wood rail and look over the moonlit bay.

But, conscious only of the man by her side, Annis remained taut and silent, sipping automatically, oblivious now to the magic of the scene.

When her glass was empty, Zan took it from her nerveless fingers. 'A refill?' he asked. She shook her head, and he replaced both glasses on the tray.

'You're very edgy,' he remarked suddenly, coming up behind her. 'I can *see* the tension in your neck and shoulders.'

As his lips brushed her vulnerable nape she flinched away and spun round. 'Don't!'

He put his hands on the veranda rail, one each side of her, effectively imprisoning her there. His eyes on her mouth, blatant seduction in his look and tone, he said softly, 'I've been waiting all day to kiss you.'

Too much pleasure was building up inside, too much wanting and aching. Feeling her self-control slipping dangerously, she said raggedly, 'I don't want you to kiss me.'

His white teeth gleamed in a smile. 'Liar.' It was obvious that in spite of her reaction earlier that day he was relatively sure of her. 'No matter what you try to tell me, you've been waiting too.'

Bending his dark head so that his lips feathered across her jaw, he whispered in her ear, 'It's terrible to hunger for something, isn't it?'

As she quivered, he drew back a little to look at her, at the smooth skin, the clear-cut features and delicate bone-structure. 'You're so lovely... All I want to do is take you to bed and make love to you until the morning.'

'And then what?' She strove to speak lightly, to sound bored, but there was a flush on her cheeks and her aquamarine eyes were brilliant, almost feverish.

'Then I'd want to start all over again. You have the ability to send me to heaven, and I'll make quite sure I take you with me...'

So quickly and deftly that she hardly knew what he was about, he began to remove the pins from her hair, allowing it to tumble down her back and over the *lei* of flowers. Then, cradling her face between his palms, he ran his fingers into the silky mass.

'You want that too...'

Gazing up at him helplessly, her pulses beating a wild tattoo, she knew it was the truth. Though in her mind she hated and rejected him, her mouth yearned for his kisses, and her body for his possession.

'And I'm going to make you admit it.'

But what her body craved, her mind must deny, even if the resultant conflict tore her apart.

It was bitterly ironic that the one man who had been able to melt the ice she'd surrounded herself with, make her want him, was also the man who had, through his uncaring disregard, destroyed not only Maya but the whole fabric of her life.

Watching her mental withdrawal, the soft mouth grow set, the expressive eyes darken with remembered sadness and pain, Zan frowned. 'What is it, Annis? What's wrong?'

'Everything,' she said jerkily. 'This "marriage", the way you forced me into it...'

He sighed, and his hands dropped to his sides. 'I should have tried a gentler, more romantic approach, but there was so much at stake...'

After a pause, as though he was trying to choose the right words, he went on, 'When you've had time to think, you'll see it's not as bad as it seems. There are compensations. Linda and Richard are secure and happy, and I could make you happy if only you'd let me...'

'I could never be happy with a man I hate.' She spat the words at him.

His face grew taut, and a white line appeared round his lips, a silent betrayal of the control he was exerting. When he made a sudden movement, she flinched away.

The threads of control stretched and grew thinner. With lethal softness, he said, 'Though I'd like to take you over my knee, I'm quite aware it wouldn't solve anything, and I don't want to put bruises on that delicate skin.'

His fingers lightly encircled her throat stroking slowly up and down while she froze, watching his face like a mesmerised rabbit.

Even when his hand slid down inside the V-neck of her blouse and made the top button pull out of the button hole, knowing he was *dangerous*, on the point of erupting out of control, she stayed quite still.

Those lean, intrusive fingers followed the valley between her breasts, exerting enough pressure to make the second button pop, then his thumb and little finger spanned from nipple to nipple beneath her flimsy bra before his palm settled over her ribcage.

Feeling the panicky thud of her heart, her absolute stillness, he asked, 'Are you afraid of me?'

Wanting to deny it, she found herself admitting, 'Yes.'

Truth proved to be her saviour.

He muttered something she didn't catch and, taking his hand away, carefully refastened the two top buttons.

As she released the breath she'd been unconsciously holding, his manner determinedly normal and friendly now, he asked, 'Would you like any supper?'

She shook her head wordlessly.

'Then shall we take a stroll along the beach before we turn in?'

Though the moment of danger seemed to have passed, she disliked and distrusted the romantic implications of a walk along the moonlit beach.

Her voice sounding thin and breathless in her own ears, she lied, 'I don't like getting sand in my shoes.'

'We'll take our shoes off.'

Zan's hand resting lightly at her waist, Annis walked a little ahead, feeling the cool brush of undergrowth against her bare legs as they made their way down the winding path.

When they reached the deserted beach they slipped off their shoes and sandals and left them by the ridged trunk of a leaning palm.

He took her hand, making her heart lurch unsteadily, and, fingers interlaced, they began to walk by the edge of the moon-silvered sea.

The sand felt smooth as warm silk under her bare feet, and the surf was cool and tingly when, with a little rush, it washed over her toes.

Gradually her tension relaxed as they strolled in silence, hand in hand, the cool, scented *leis* they were wearing completely in tune with the tropical night.

At the far point a dark, rocky outcrop stretched dragon-like into the water. For a while they sat, their backs against the warm rock, enjoying the balmy air, before starting homewards. As they approached the sloping palm, Zan moved a little ahead to retrieve their footwear. Looking up into the dark sky where a warm wind was blowing the stars about, Annis sighed at the beauty of the tropical night.

The sigh was still on her lips when she stubbed her toe against a half-buried piece of driftwood and stumbled.

With a quick movement Zan turned and caught her against his chest. Off balance, she lay against him. He was like the rock, strong and unyielding, yet her soft, womanly curves fitted against his hard male frame like two pieces of interlocking jigsaw.

Fire raced through her, swift and all-consuming, filling her body with a wanton heat.

Holding her against him, so the *leis* were crushed between them, he tilted her chin and looked down at her.

Her eyes were wide and alarmed, her lips trembled. But when he bent his dark head to kiss her they parted beneath his touch, and as though there was no help for it, her arms crept up across his broad shoulders to wind around his neck. His hands shaped her slender hips and held her firmly against his lower body. She was only vaguely conscious of the intimacy of the contact because all her attention was focused on the invasion of his mouth.

She was bemused and enslaved when he finally lifted his head and set his lips to chase chills down the side of her neck and linger at the base of her throat and the warm hollows of her shoulderbones.

'Do you want me to make love to you?'

The whispered words brought a rude awakening, and passion shut off like dousing a light.

'No!'

At her strangled cry he paused, then began to trail kisses back up the path he had just traced downwards, bent on recapturing her mouth, hoping to repair the tear his whispered question had made in the web of sensual enchantment he was spinning around her.

Realising his intention, she buried her face in his shoulder, moving her head in negation.

His hands began to stroke her back, gently, soothingly. When she relaxed slightly, he eased her away from him and tilted her chin to look into her cloudy eyes. 'No...' she said again.

Unable to hide the rueful twist to his lips, he murmured, 'Perhaps I need a sense of timing even more than a store of patience. Ah, well...'

He retrieved her sandals, and going down on his haunches took a folded handkerchief from his pocket and brushed the sand from her slender foot, before slipping them on.

His own shoes and socks he tucked under one arm and walked back barefooted, while she moved beside him like someone in a trance.

When they reached the house they went straight upstairs. All the luggage, she found, had been put in the bedroom overlooking the sea.

Recoiling, she said raggedly, 'If you think I'm going to share your bed——'

'I don't.' Zan's interruption was curt. 'If we shared a bed I wouldn't be able to keep my hands off you. But Hiawa would never have believed that a newly married couple might want to sleep apart.'

He came towards her. Her face half lifted in anticipation, the breath caught in her throat, she waited.

Black head bent, he seemed to hesitate fractionally, then he straightened, and picking up his case, went out, the door clicking shut behind him softly but decisively.

For a few moment she stood quite still, staring at the closed door. Then, taking off the bruised *lei*, she unpacked her nightdress and prepared for bed, all the time trying to stifle a hollow feeling of disappointment.

How could she feel so lost, so empty, just because a man she hated had gone without kissing her? After the traumas of the evening, she should have felt pleased and relieved, delighted that she'd been able to get rid of him so speedily.

It was this inability to control her emotions that she found so frightening. This terrible pull between what she *felt* and what she *ought* to feel.

Her mind was at war with her body and the conflict seemed likely to destroy her. Just the fact that she wanted him was a rent in the fabric of her self-respect. And she *did* want him.

She knew with sickening certainty that out there on the beach, if he hadn't spoken when he had, just laid her on the sand, she would have forgotten her hatred, forgotten about Maya, and rendered him passion for passion.

How could she be so stupid, so *weak*? She flayed herself until she felt raw and bleeding.

Next morning she awoke to hot sunshine and an icy determination to stay in control. She must make sure they were alone as little as possible, and when they were alone keep him at arm's length.

Of course it would have been much easier if she hadn't once surrendered to him. The fact that she had had undermined her whole campaign of resistance, and given him renewed hope.

Given him justification for his patience.

And he had patience. But he also had a primitive sensuality, a ruthless purpose, and when his patience came to an end and he was still thwarted, instead of letting her go, as he'd promised, would he take what she refused to give?

No, surely not. She believed he'd keep his word. She *had* to believe it.

But one thing was crystal-clear. She had been right to doubt her ability to lead him on for the satisfaction of ultimately rejecting him. It was far too risky. Now if he made any move to make love to her she would freeze him off immediately and keep freezing him off until his patience was finally exhausted.

But Zan gave her no chance to put her decision into practice. It soon became plain that he'd gone back to being the friendly companion he'd been during those days in San Francisco.

With one difference only. Now he didn't kiss her goodnight.

The deliberate omission unsettled and worried her. Was it that he dared not trust himself? Or did he no longer want to?

No, she couldn't believe that was the case. Though he disguised it well, every so often when he looked at her there was a tiny lick of white-hot flame that told her his desire was still burning fiercely.

In the days that followed, he showed her everything, from the excitement and bustle of exotic Waikiki and Honolulu to the moving environment of Pearl Harbour, and the spectacular Pali Cliffs where King Kamehameha—the first ruler to unite the Hawaiian Islands—had driven his enemies over the thousand-foot drop.

She found that sophistication vied with simplicity, crowded beaches with quiet coves, native shops with trendy boutiques, and traditional Polynesian-type fare with American fast food.

After the first strenuous week of sightseeing, Zan quietly, unobtrusively began to slow down the pace, interspersing picnics, swimming, and more leisurely days spent on the beach.

Resolutely shutting out all the anxieties waiting like vultures to beset her, Annis enjoyed it all, including the hot tropical sun.

Unlike most true blondes she tanned easily, without freckling or burning, and her pale skin turned to a becoming clear gold.

Even when heat gripped the Island like a sweaty fist, she never looked hot and sticky and crumpled, as did a lot of the less fortunate women.

One afternoon when they were in Honolulu, with the sun beating down and the pavements throwing back an oven heat, they stopped to have a drink at an open-air café. Ignoring the shade of a palm-thatched umbrella, Annis chose instead a place in the sun.

Watching her sitting there, coolly elegant despite the heat, a strange note in his voice, Zan remarked, 'You are the most amazing woman I've ever met. Even the Hawaiian sun seems unable to melt that Snow Queen image, that cool perfection.'

Softly, he added, 'Yet you have such a passionate mouth. It's fascinated me right from the start, that combination of fire and ice.'

She had often wondered what Zan saw in her. Now, the way he spoke, and the glint in his eyes, made the tiny hairs on the back of her neck rise.

While they did some shopping and picked up tickets for the *luau* Zan was taking her to that evening, his words stayed in the forefront of her mind.

Back at Lani House, when she began to shower and change for the *luau*, they were still echoing through her head. *Fire and ice...*

After the comparative calm of the past three weeks, she all at once felt jumpy and unsettled. Telling herself not to be a fool, she selected a white sleeveless dress with a slim skirt and a halter neck and matched its navy trim with navy sandals.

She was in her undies, her light make-up already applied, brushing out her long flaxen hair when, from nowhere, came a clear memory of Zan's bedroom at Griffin House.

The room she had thought almost spartan in its cool, elegant simplicity, until she'd seen the Spanish dancer, passionate and sensuous, in a dress like flame. *Fire and ice...*

Realising she matched the room, she felt curiously shaken. Shaken too to find he had guessed so accurately what sensuality and passion lay beneath her cool exterior. She hoped he hadn't also guessed how, since her surrender in San Francisco, she had lain awake night after night with a relentless gnawing ache inside.

When the body craved and the mind denied, the resultant conflict could be fierce. Her body, newly awakened to passion, had refused to go meekly back to innocence.

Only the thought of Maya, and the revenge she'd planned, had enabled her mind to master her rebellious body and keep her outwardly cool.

Fire and ice . . .

She was standing in front of the dressing-table, about to pin her hair into its usual sleek chignon, when she paused to study the reflection gazing back at her. The patrician face looked beautiful and aloof, coldly perfect, except for that tell-tale mouth.

Suddenly, savagely, she wanted to destroy that fire and ice image which Zan seemed to find so fascinating.

Going back into the bathroom, she scrubbed her face until it shone, and plaited her hair into a single thick flaxen rope which she fastened with a stray rubber band from her bag.

Then, deciding to go the whole hog, she put on a pair of jeans and a baggy T-shirt with a fat pink hippo cavorting on it. A holiday present from the twins, which she'd dutifully packed without intending to wear.

Taking another look at her reflection, she saw with grim satisfaction that in two minutes flat she'd changed from a coldly passionate Snow Queen into an escapee from the fourth form.

Except that no self-respecting fourth-former would have been seen dead looking so rustic.

As the old proverb insisted, there was more than one way to kill a cat. If Zan wanted her for that combination of cool sophistication and latent passion, he was in for an unpleasant surprise.

'About ready?' his voice broke into her thoughts.

'Coming,' she called, and, anticipating his shock, hugged herself.

If he was startled, he hid it well.

His well-shaped head of shorn black curls tilted to one side, his eyes ironic, he studied the ridiculous T-shirt, her shiny nose and artless plait. 'Why the metamorphosis?'

Innocently, she queried, 'Don't you like it?'

'So it was done for *my* benefit?'

'No, mine.'

'Whichever, I definitely approve.'

She was wondering uneasily whether his enthusiasm was genuine when, with more than a touch of silky menace, he went on, 'It adds another dimension to your character. Opens up all kinds of interesting possibilities now the Snow Queen is no longer in evidence.'

Chills running up and down her spine, she tried to look unconcerned and failed abysmally.

'Come on, then, Pollyanna.' Smiling tigerishly, Zan picked up her plait, and gave it a tug. 'Incidentally, I love the pigtail.'

Ignoring both his smile and his words, suddenly afraid she'd made a terrible mistake, she followed him out to the car.

During the ride up the coast to Kawaia, where the *luau*—a native orgy of food, drink and entertainment—was being held, both apparently busy with their thoughts, they spoke little.

Over the past days their silences had been easy, companionable, but this time they crackled with a sexual tension that made Annis's nerves feel like overstretched fabric.

When they reach Kawaia, the wide sandy beach was all excitement and bustle, with flaming torches and colourful native costumes and dozens of holidaymakers out to enjoy the evening.

Leis were given in a traditional welcome, then everyone took their seats on wooden benches drawn up to long trestle-tables loaded with flowers and exotic Hawaiian dishes.

As soon as Annis was installed on one of the benches, Zan took a seat by her side, far too close for comfort, the firm warmth of his thigh touching hers, making her heartbeat grow fast and erratic.

The entertainment—fire-eating, hula dancing, singing, and a group of Hawaiian ladies with long flowered dresses and *leis* playing banjos—was colourful and amusing.

Annis smiled and clapped with the rest, and drank some of the sweet white wine, but her appetite had quite deserted her.

Zan's tawny eyes never missed a thing. 'You'd better have some food, or you won't have strength to fight,' he said cryptically.

She made no reply, but, aware of his mocking surveillance, managed to eat a small plate of seafood and some fresh fruit salad.

When the time came to go, she was both relieved and reluctant, nervously aware of a new sense of purpose in his manner. Aware that the period of calm was over and a new assault was imminent.

He drove back in silence and followed her into the house. She'd been hoping to escape straight to her room but, his arm around her waist, he propelled her down the stairs saying, 'I'll make some coffee.'

About to argue, she bit her lip. An impassive acceptance might be the best defence. It was far less challenging. And Zan was a man who thrived on challenge.

While she sat quiet and watchful, he made a pot of coffee with deft efficiency.

On edge, wary, she accepted and drank a cup of coffee she didn't want. Then, unable to stand the suspense a moment longer, she stood up abruptly and, turning away, said, 'I'm going to bed now.'

Lean fingers encircled her wrist, keeping her there while he stood looking down at her.

Against her will her gaze was drawn to his. The gleam in his tawny eyes jolted her, putting her in mind of a cat contemplating a saucer of cream.

Softly, he said, 'I haven't kissed you goodnight.'

'But you don't...you don't kiss me goodnight any longer.'

'Well, tonight I have a mind to.' Quite gently, but with unshakeable purpose, he took her face between his palms.

Smiling down at her, he stroked his thumbs gently, seductively, over her high cheekbones.

While she stood wide-eyed, hypnotised by that sensuous, caressing movement, he slowly bent his dark head and began to woo her with soft, beguiling kisses.

Light as thistledown, his lips closed her lids and touched the wildly beating pulse at her temples, before following the curve of her cheek to linger enticingly at the corner of her mouth.

When they finally settled on hers she was so bewitched and breathless that it scarcely needed the brush of his tongue-tip to coax them to part.

While his mouth was exploring hers, his fingers were busy undoing the plait, running through the long, silky hair to her waist, then up beneath the baggy T-shirt to release the front fastening of her light bra.

She gasped as his hands found her breasts, a finger and thumb teasing each nipple so they firmed beneath his touch.

The exquisite, needle-sharp sensations he was sending through her served to heat the blood in her veins and made her burn as though with fever.

As she shuddered and whimpered, his arms closed around her and, the flower *leis* crushed between them, he kissed her with a passionate need that found its counterpart in her hunger for him.

Lost to everything but the desire he was arousing in her, she made no objection when the deft hands undressed her, and the strong arms carried her up the short flight of stairs to the moonlit bedroom that overlooked the bay.

Turning back the thin coverlet, he laid her on the big divan bed and sat on the edge looking down at her, alluring as the island goddess Pele, with her long silky hair and the *lei* of flowers still adorning her bare breasts.

Then, his hands moving slowly, seductively over her slender body, he kissed her lips, before letting his mouth follow where his hands had already awakened a torment of delight.

The windows were open wide, and a night breeze drifted in, fanning her heated skin. Perhaps it was that breeze which served to dispel some of the mists of passion and bring back a breath of sanity.

But even with the return to sanity she seemed incapable of saving herself, unable to break free. It was as though, mind and body, she was under his spell, her whole being held in thrall.

A bondage she had to break before it was too late.

If she allowed herself to be seduced just one more time she would be destroyed, torn apart by the ambivalence of her feelings. On one hand this fatal attraction; on the other, the knowledge that she was betraying everything she'd once held dear.

Lying quite still, she forced herself to think of Maya and her father, of the home she'd loved.

Like switching off a heat source, the fiery excitement died, her skin took on a glacial chill and the very blood in her veins seemed to turn to ice.

He knew at once.

'Ouch!' Removing his hands, he looked at the palms. As her gaze followed his, he said laconically, 'Frostbite.'

When she ignored his attempt at levity, he asked, 'What's wrong, Annis?'

Clearly, she said, 'I don't want to sleep with you.'

'But you *do*.' His hands closed around the soft flesh of her upper arms.

She shook her head. 'That night in San Francisco was a terrible mistake I have no intention of repeating. I despise myself for it.'

In the moonlight she saw his eyes blaze. Baffled and infuriated by her continued stand, his grip tightened until she almost cried out with pain.

'You're hurting me,' she said through stiff lips.

After a moment that savage grip relaxed, and he shook his head as if to clear it.

Then, as though he'd decided on a gentle approach, the anger was wiped from his face. 'Well, talk to me,' he coaxed. 'Tell me why you feel that way.'

Anger she could have coped with, but tenderness, she knew all too well, might prove to be her undoing. Sitting up with a jerk, she made an effort at finality. 'There's no point in talking about it.'

'I need to know, Annis.'

She shook her head. 'I just want to forget the whole thing.'

'How can you forget the unforgettable?' His voice grew softer and deeper as he drew her into his arms.

Dreadfully afraid that if he kissed her again she would be lost, she put her palms against his chest and made an attempt to push him away. 'Leave me alone,' she cried. 'You promised you wouldn't force me.'

Letting her go, he drew back. 'I didn't force you then. You came to me willingly, eagerly, if you remember.'

Dragging the bedspread up to cover her nakedness, she said fiercely, 'I don't want to remember. I wish it had never happened.'

'*Why*?' he asked with urgency. Then, as though wanting to read her expression, he reached for the pull cord, flooding the room with light. 'Tell me why you wish that.'

'Because I loathe and detest you for what you've done to me and my family.'

'I wish to God I'd never used strong-arm methods,' he admitted. 'But when you told me Leighton was your lover, I saw red. I couldn't bear to think of you in his arms, in his bed . . . That's what made me lose my head and rush into things, when I should have tried time and patience.'

'No amount of time or patience——'

'I don't believe that,' he interrupted. 'But we'll see, shall we? I still have the best part of a year to make you change your mind.'

Like a handful of stinging gravel, she threw the words in his face. 'A lifetime wouldn't be long enough.'

CHAPTER SEVEN

Two days later they started for home, landing at Heathrow late on a Saturday morning. Spring, though cool, was in full bloom, and London was looking its vibrant best.

When they reached Griffin House, Mrs Matheson, advised of their return by phone, was waiting to greet them. If she thought they were strangely quiet for returning honeymooners, she kept it to herself, asking merely, 'Will you be wanting something to eat now?'

'No, thanks,' Zan said. 'We had an early lunch on the plane.'

'Well, if it's all right by you, I was hoping to spend the weekend with my sister as usual?'

'Yes, of course. You get off.' His hard face sardonic, he added, 'I've a wife now to pander to my needs.'

He carried the luggage upstairs and, without asking, put Annis's case in the bedroom she'd used before the wedding.

At the door, he turned to say, 'When I've had a shower, I intend to go into the office... Unless you need me?'

She looked him in the face, her eyes full of silent derision, and was oddly discomfited when a dark flush appeared along his cheekbones.

Without a word he left, closing the door behind him with a kind of finality.

Since he'd walked out of her room the night of the *luau* he'd been civil, but distant, seldom looking at her and speaking only when necessary. Ignoring the strange feeling of loss, the ache of regret that refused to go away, she'd told herself how pleased she was. That so long as she could keep him at a distance she would be happy.

But now she wondered, would she? It was as though she couldn't hurt him without hurting herself.

She had finished unpacking and was about to take a shower, when she heard his light footsteps returning down the corridor.

On an impulse, she opened her door and asked, 'What time will you want dinner?'

He looked surprised, then, his voice cool, dismissive, answered, 'I expect to be working late, so I'll probably eat out.'

Calling herself all kinds of a fool for feeling wounded because he'd refused the olive branch she'd held out, Annis went to take a shower. Knowing she was far too restless to catch up on lost sleep, and unwilling to sit around twiddling her thumbs, she changed into a smart spring suit and set off to visit Linda and Richard.

They were delighted to see her. Linda's first question was, 'Isn't Zan with you?'

'He's gone into the office,' Annis answered lightly. 'You know what men are.'

'Is he coming along later?'

'No... I only popped in for an hour or so.'

'Just back from honeymoon—I expect they want the evening to themselves,' Richard said with a grin.

'Talking of honeymoons...you've got a terrific tan!' Linda exclaimed enviously. 'Though the weather hasn't been bad here, beside you Richard and I still look winter-pale.'

'Winter-pale' they might be, but Annis's heart lifted to see them both apparently fit and happy, and she could only give fervent thanks that so far things seemed to have worked out well for them. If not for herself.

'How's the arm now?' she asked. 'I see the plaster's off.'

'It's nearly as good as new.' Linda turned her wrist to show the degree of movement. 'Though I don't know how I'd manage without Mrs Sheldon. She's an absolute treasure. She's taken all the children off to Diana's first birthday party... Diana is our neighbour's little girl——'

'Oh by the way,' Richard butted in on the domestic details, 'thanks for the postcards...'

During the time away, Annis had phoned periodically to assure herself that everything was all right, and scrawled one or two hasty cards.

'But they only whetted our appetite, so tell us all about Hawaii...'

It was well after six before Annis, knowing that to linger any longer might make them wonder, said reluctantly that she'd have to go.

'Sure you can't stay for a meal?' Linda asked.

'Quite sure.'

'That's a pity,' Richard remarked, as they accompanied her to the door. 'Stephen said he might drop in and take pot luck...

'By the way, he seemed positively stunned when I told him you were married. So much so that I half wondered if he was carrying a torch for you...'

Linda gave Annis a parting hug. 'Now don't forget, as soon as you and Zan feel like socialising, come and have dinner with us.'

The evening was mild and sunny, the sky cloudless. Feeling restless, and in no hurry to get back to an empty house, Annis decided to walk.

Deep in thought, she didn't notice the blue Cavalier that had drawn into the kerb until a window rolled down and a familiar voice called, 'Annis...'

'Stephen... Hello...' She smiled at him with genuine warmth.

'Annis...' he said again. Then, almost stammering, 'H-how nice to see you...'

'It's nice to see you.' And it was. Ordinary, kind, uncomplicated Stephen. A man she was at home with, who didn't set her heart pounding or quicken her breathing, who posed no threat.

His ears turning red, he told her, 'I was on my way to visit Linda and Richard.'

'I've just left. Richard mentioned that you might be dropping in.'

'Yes, I... Look, are you in a hurry? I mean, do you have to get back?'

'Well, no...'

'I-I'd like to talk to you. Please...' He looked almost desperate. 'What about dinner at Sunter's? I was planning to take you somewhere special as soon as you were over your flu. But then I had to make an urgent business trip, and when I got back... Look, I've just *got* to talk to you...'

Suddenly realising what she might be letting herself in for, but feeling she owed him some kind of explanation, she answered unwillingly, 'All right,' and climbed into the car.

A little way up the street from Sunter's, a parking meter was free. It was still early and the quiet, select restaurant was almost empty. They were shown to a table for two in an alcove, and handed leather-covered menus.

Made uneasy by the realisation that the imposing building which housed AP Worldwide's offices was barely a block away, Annis chose hurriedly, not caring what she ate.

As soon as the waiter had departed with their order, Stephen burst out raggedly, 'Why didn't you *tell* me you were going to be married?'

'Well, it all happened so suddenly,' she said helplessly.

'I don't understand why you married *him* of all people.' Almost accusingly, Stephen added, 'You told me you didn't even like him.'

'At first I didn't. But then...' Not knowing what to say, she hesitated.

'He was interested in you that very first night. Even before he came over I noticed he was watching you. In fact he hardly took his eyes off you...

'I should have known he was up to something when he offered me those damned tickets. But I never imagined...' Stephen broke off as the waiter returned with the first course.

When they were alone again, he asked gloomily, 'I suppose he swept you off your feet?'

'Yes, you could say that.'

Suddenly, violently, he said, 'That's what I should have done. I've loved you for *ages*... I was hoping you'd marry *me* one day...'

'Oh, Stephen, I'm sorry.' Impulsively she took his hand and gave it a squeeze. 'But even if...if things had been different, I couldn't have married you.'

He gripped her hand almost painfully. 'But you made me think you liked me. You said you preferred me to Zan Power... I should have known you didn't mean it.'

'When I said it, I *did* mean it,' she assured him. 'I've always been fond of you. But fondness isn't enough. I've never loved anyone enough to want to marry them...'

'Until *he* came along... Well, I suppose I can't blame you for falling for him; he's got it all. I just wish things could have been different. I wish I could have been the one to sweep you off your feet...'

Stephen, with his usual dogged persistence, went over the same ground again and again. It was almost eight-thirty before Annis could escape, and by that time the restaurant was full.

Suddenly afraid of the consequences if Zan should happen to see them together, she insisted on going home by taxi.

As he put her into it, she said awkwardly, 'It might be best if you don't tell anyone we've had dinner together.'

Catching on with unusual quickness, Stephen said bitterly, 'You've no need to worry, he's not likely to be jealous of *me*.'

That's all *you* know, Annis thought, as the taxi drew away.

When she reached Griffin House it was dark and silent. Clearly Zan hadn't yet returned. Hardly knowing whether to be pleased or sorry, she went straight to bed. Though she was utterly weary, she found herself listening for him, unable to sleep. It was the early hours of the morning before she heard the front door open and close, and his step on the stairs.

Next day it was almost noon when she awoke. The house was quiet and, instinct told her, empty. Surely he wasn't working all weekend?

She pulled on a skirt and top and, her hair in a ponytail, went down to the kitchen. Having made some coffee and a cheese sandwich, unable to settle to anything, she tried to immerse herself in the Sunday papers.

Still she was jumpy, on edge, listening for every sound, waiting for something to happen. No, not for something to happen, for Zan to come home.

It was well after six when she finally heard his key in the lock and hurried into the hall.

He looked tired was her first thought, like a man who'd driven himself too fast and too far. He also looked as if he was quietly, but *lethally*, angry. There was a grim purpose in his manner, a controlled urgency that almost crackled.

Trying to hide her anxiety, she asked, 'What time would you like dinner?'

'We're eating out,' he said curtly. 'A foursome. I've arranged to be at Helen's by seven-thirty.'

'Oh,' she said without enthusiasm, feeling headachy and depressed and anything but sociable.

The look he gave her chilled her to the marrow. 'You sound as if you don't like Helen?'

'As a matter of fact, I do. I like her very much.'

'I'm glad about that,' he said sardonically. 'I wouldn't want your prejudices to spill over.'

Without another word, he turned away.

Seeing nothing else for it, Annis followed him up the stairs to shower and change.

Her blonde hair in a smooth coil, she added a touch of mascara to her long, gold-tipped lashes, and a pale gloss to her lips, before stepping into a slim-skirted black dress which looked wonderful with her golden tan. A light spray of Rive Gauche and she was ready.

Though she'd been quick, Zan was waiting in the hall. Freshly shaven, his black curls still slightly damp, he looked impeccable in a dark, lightweight suit with an ivory silk shirt and a tie with swirls of muted colour.

Though on the surface he now appeared more relaxed, Annis judged that, in reality, he remained taut as a drawn bowstring.

Whatever had been bugging him still was.

When they reached Elwood Place, Helen's housekeeper opened the door. A moment later Helen herself appeared and greeted him warmly, before turning to address a laughing word to someone behind her.

Only when the man followed her on to the pavement did Annis realise that it wasn't Matt but Stephen.

Shock made her mouth go dry and the smile of greeting freeze on her face.

'Hi,' Helen said cheerfully as she climbed into the back of the car, followed by Stephen. 'I gather you liked Hawaii... Zan says you can stand the heat...which is just as well.' Then, without pause, 'What did you think of San Francisco?'

'Loved it,' Annis managed through stiff lips.

'Matt's over there at the moment on a flying visit,' Helen told her, 'so Stephen has kindly agreed to be my escort.'

'Mr Power rang and asked——' Stephen began.

'We're away from the office,' Zan interrupted, as he slid behind the wheel, 'so we can dispense with formality.'

Obviously gratified, Stephen resumed, 'Zan rang and asked me to make up a foursome...'

For *asked* read *ordered*, Annis thought bitterly.

'Of course I was delighted...'

Why had Zan engineered this foursome? she wondered, alarm spreading through her like smoke through a burning house.

Aware that he never did anything without a good reason, she feared for Stephen. Though she knew that Stephen's comfortably prosaic appearance was belied by a sharp, not to say brilliant brain where electronics were concerned, when it came to dealing with a man of Zan's calibre he was like a child in the company of a tiger.

Glancing at Zan's dark, formidable profile, she hid a shiver of apprehension. Whatever he might be planning, her only defence seemed to be an icy composure.

That composure was badly shaken when they drew up outside Sunter's.

Annis was careful not to glance in Stephen's direction as they were ushered to a table on the edge of the tiny dance-floor.

Apparently intent on making the evening a festive one, Zan asked for champagne before going on to order lavishly.

The food, when it came, was excellent, the champagne vintage. As far as Annis was concerned it could have been bread and water.

While the meal progressed they discussed a wide range of topics, before going on to job losses and the effects of the recession.

For the most part Annis listened, leaving it mainly to Helen and Stephen, both animated talkers.

But it was soon clear that Zan, though saying appreciably less than the other two, was the one who controlled the conversation.

He was a born manipulator, she thought grimly, and they were merely puppets.

Only when he purposefully introduced the subject of redundancies in the companies he owned did she suddenly see with blinding clarity *why* he'd arranged this evening.

Somehow he *knew* she'd had dinner with Stephen. That was what had been bugging him.

Biting her inner lip until she tasted blood, Annis admitted it was all her fault. She should never have agreed.

Now, for something so petty, Zan was going to set about destroying Stephen. Poor, innocent Stephen...

She gripped her wine glass until the delicate stem was in danger of snapping, wanting desperately to say something, to tell Zan the meeting had been accidental and quite innocent.

But the expression on his face told her with certainty that even if he believed her, and that was doubtful, it was too late to deflect him from his purpose.

Poised for the kill, his beautiful mouth ruthless, Zan met her burning gaze with a glint of pure steel before turning back to the younger man.

'My biggest headache with regard to the middle management strata,' he continued evenly, 'quite often proves to be that I've too many chiefs and not enough indians...

'Your team have been doing some really excellent work, but I already have a central think-tank... Now the indians can be successfully amalgamated, but I won't need two chiefs...'

Lulled into a false sense of security, happily unaware of the suspended axe, Stephen waited eagerly as his boss went on, 'My own head of department, who's been with me for years, is a very good man and I'd hate to lose him. He's also married, with a young child and another on the way...'

Zan paused, before adding deliberately, 'Which means, I'm afraid, that *you* will have to be the one to go.'

Surprise in her lovely sherry-coloured eyes, Helen stared at her brother. While Annis, her slim hands clenched in fists of impotent rage, was engulfed by a tide of hatred so strong she felt sick.

His round, chubby face blank with shock, his mouth hanging foolishly open, Stephen sat quite still.

'However,' Zan continued blandly, 'you're much too valuable to lose entirely, so I have a suggestion to make...

'Blair's communications set-up in Santa Clara, better known as Silicon Valley, need a man with your kind of brains and ability...you've already made quite a few business trips out to California, so you know the ropes, which is invaluable. They want someone to go out to installations not only in the States, but Central and South America, the West Indies, anywhere in that part of the globe...

'I've already mentioned your name to them, and the job's yours if you want it...and don't mind living in the Golden State.' The last was added jokingly.

In the background a small dance orchestra started to play, 'Do You Know The Way To San Jose?'

Zan smiled, relishing the irony, before going on, 'It means a big step up the ladder, a much higher salary, and far greater freedom.'

His ears glowing like rubies, Stephen burst out eagerly, 'It sounds fantastic! Don't you think so, Annis?'

She couldn't have said a word to save herself from the scaffold.

Catching her eye, Zan smiled like a tiger and added, 'They want a kind of troubleshooter who's able to get up and go at a moment's notice. And they need someone who can start immediately.'

'By *immediately* you mean...?'

'A seat's been booked on tomorrow's plane. When I spoke to you earlier you mentioned your American visa is still valid, and this will be classed as a business trip until you can obtain the necessary clearance.' Briskly, he went on, 'I believe you're still living with your parents?'

'That's right,' Stephen admitted.

'So you'll have no problems property-wise?'

'No, but I...' Thrown by the suddenness of it, Stephen stopped and gave Annis a helpless look.

'As you two are old friends,' Zan said smoothly, 'perhaps you'd like a chance to discuss it?'

The orchestra had changed to a Cole Porter classic, and, turning to Helen, he asked, 'Would you care to dance?'

'Love to.' She rose to her feet with a smile, a confident woman at ease with this formidable man.

Annis watched the pair take to the crowded floor with a strange feeling of detachment.

They made an impressive couple. Both black-haired, both olive-skinned, both with that extra something—glamour, charisma, sex-appeal, call it what you would—that set certain people apart.

Becoming aware that Stephen was talking, Annis dragged her gaze away and gave him her attention.

'...It's come so out of the blue... I suppose it's knocked me sideways. But it's just the kind of opportunity I've dreamt of. A *troubleshooter*...' There was excitement in his voice, and his eyes were alight. 'I've always wanted to travel, to have that kind of interesting, *colourful* job instead of just boring routine.'

Annis was staggered. She'd never guessed what a fiery, romantic nature lay beneath his commonplace, somewhat dull exterior. But it helped to explain his admiration for his boss.

It also explained why Zan—who had clearly read him much better than she had—had offered him such an inducement.

'If you feel like that, it makes sense to take it,' she said firmly.

'I'm glad you think so,' Zan remarked with grim satisfaction.

Startled, she looked up and met those icy green-gold eyes. What she read in them made her shiver and glance hastily away.

He waited courteously until Helen was seated before resuming his own chair. Then, turning to the younger man, he asked, 'So what's your answer?'

Stephen squared his shoulders. 'I'd like the job.'

Zan nodded approval and said briskly, 'Be in the MD's office tomorrow morning at ten-thirty. I'll have all the necessary paperwork ready and fill you in on the details.'

Mission accomplished, he apparently saw no reason to linger. Within minutes the bill was paid and they were on their way.

Stephen had left his car at Elwood Place, so Zan took them both back to Helen's.

'Coming in for a coffee?' she asked, as they drew up outside.

'No, thanks,' Zan refused. Curling a hand around Annis's nape, he added softly, 'I'm planning on us having an early night.'

It was a barely concealed threat that chilled her blood and sent shivers chasing through her.

Somehow she found her voice and said to Stephen, 'I hope you have a good journey... Make all those dreams come true.'

When the pair alighted, after saying their goodbyes and thanks for a lovely evening, Helen tucked a companionable arm through Stephen's and asked, '*You'll* have a coffee before you go, won't you?'

As soon as the car door slammed, without a word, Zan turned the wheel and drove away.

After one surreptitious peep at the cold, ruthless mask of his face, Annis stared straight ahead and, biting her lip, tried not to give way to the threatening panic.

While he garaged the car she let herself in and hung up her coat. She wanted desperately to run, to lock herself in her room. But in the mood he was in he might easily break down the door. And if he was once driven to violence there was no knowing where it might end...

Shivering, she went through to the kitchen, facing the fact that a confrontation was inevitable. But he wouldn't *hurt* her, she told herself firmly.

When she glanced up to find him standing silently in the doorway, watching her with hooded eyes, she was no longer quite so sure.

Annis had never lacked courage, and now, in extremity, deciding attack was the best means of defence, she lifted her chin and asked, 'How did you know?'

'I'd gone to have a meal at Sunter's when I saw you there together.' Flatly, he added, 'I decided that for everyone's sake, not least his own, he had to go.'

'Well, congratulations! He's gone, or as good as... And where has it got you? What have you actually achieved?'

He came towards her, tall and lean and dangerous. 'You tell me.'

'Absolutely nothing!'

'Oh, a little more than that, I think,' he disagreed. 'At the very least I've cleared the decks.'

'And in record time,' she said with undisguised rancour. 'Short of using a magic wand, you couldn't have got rid of him faster.'

Then, voicing the additional worry that had been lurking at the back of her mind, 'I suppose after a short interval they'll get rid of him just as fast.'

'Not if he can do the job,' Zan answered coldly. 'And I believe he can. In fact I rather think it will suit him to perfection.'

'A fat lot you'd care if it didn't. You've deprived him of a good, safe position, turned his life upside down, and it wasn't even necessary.'

'Oh, it was necessary, believe me,' Zan said grimly. 'Once I knew he was meeting my wife behind my back...'

She flinched at the venom in his voice.

'Look,' she said desperately, 'I realise now it was a silly thing to do, but it wasn't *planned*. He was going to see Linda and Richard as I was coming away. We had a meal together, that's all. It was quite innocent.'

'He was holding your hand.' Zan's voice cut like a whiplash.

'No, *I* was holding *his*.' She saw Zan's eyes flash as she set the record straight. 'I just felt sorry for the way I'd treated him,' she added shakily. Then with a flash of spirit, 'If you thought something was going on, I'm surprised you didn't come over...'

Dispassionately, Zan said, 'I couldn't trust myself not to kill him. I had to walk the streets until I'd got myself under control and could think of some more civilised way of dealing with him.'

'Why didn't you just fire him?' she asked curiously. 'Why go to all the trouble of finding him another job?'

'Just firing him wouldn't have served my purpose. I prefer to have him six thousand miles away.' With biting self-derision, he added, 'And I didn't want you to hate me any more than you already do.'

'That would be impossible,' she told him sweetly, and heard his teeth grind together.

'Well, hate me or not,' he said coldly, 'tonight you're sharing my bed. From now on this marriage is going to be a real one.'

'No!' Her voice high and frightened, she said, 'That's breaking the terms of our agreement.'

He looked at her coldly. 'But you've already broken them.'

Her blood seemed to freeze in her veins. Just for that innocent meeting, for holding hands, he'd dealt ruthlessly with Stephen. Now his icy anger was directed against her, and she was going to have to pay.

'Oh, please...' she begged.

He smiled tigerishly. 'I intend to...'

She stood quite still trying desperately to get her thoughts into some kind of order, but they were tumbled, chaotic, like a kaleidoscope being turned so quickly that no clear pattern could emerge.

'Well, Annis? Are you coming willingly? Or do I have to carry you?'

It would be useless trying to fight him, she knew. He was quite determined, and so much stronger than she was. A passive resistance might prove to be her best, maybe her only defence.

Head high, she preceded him up the stairs and into his bedroom.

When he followed her in, she turned to face him. She expected him to take her in his arms and kiss her, but, leaning his back against the panels, a cruel little smile on his lips, he suggested, 'Suppose you get undressed?'

When, eyes widening, she stared mutely at him, he said with bitter mockery, 'You were prepared to hold another man's hand because you felt sorry for the way you'd treated him. After the way you've treated *me*, I figure you owe me a great deal more...'

'You're just trying to humiliate me, to make me feel ashamed... indecent,' she charged breathlessly.

'Now why would I want to do that?'

When she stayed mute, his voice silky, he added, 'And really it's quite *decent* for a wife to strip for her husband...even if, at the same time, it proves to be thoroughly erotic.'

A shade wildly she fought back. 'If it's eroticism you're looking for, a husband stripping for his wife could prove just as erotic.'

He laughed suddenly, white teeth gleaming. 'Well, I'm a firm believer in the equality of the sexes...' His eyes holding hers, he began to undo the knot in his tie.

CHAPTER EIGHT

STANDING rooted to the spot, Annis watched as though hypnotised while he pulled the tie free of his collar and, having tossed it aside, started to slowly unbutton his shirt.

Smiling a little, his movements full of masculine grace, yet oddly threatening, he eased it from its waistband and discarded it.

When his hands moved to unfasten his trousers and slide them over lean hips, her mouth went desert-dry, and as his dark silk briefs followed she swallowed convulsively.

Wide-shouldered and narrow-hipped, bronzed skin gleaming like oiled silk, he was as magnificent as some Greek god, only the area of paler skin that had been covered by his briefs betraying a more modern civilisation.

Wanting to look away, but unable, she felt her nipples tingle and firm betrayingly beneath the thin silky material of her black dress.

'You were quite right,' he said softly, significantly.

Her eyes lifted to his face, to find he was studying the clear evidence of her arousal with more than a hint of triumph.

She longed to fold her arms over her breasts, but a kind of perverse pride kept her chin high and her hands by her sides.

'Your turn now,' he commanded.

When she made no move to obey, he suggested, 'Or would you rather I did it for you?'

Resisting the panicky urge to back away, she forced herself to stand silent and unresisting while he took the pins from her hair and let the heavy silken mass tumble around her shoulders.

Then, his fingers having dealt unhurriedly with the zip, he slid the black dress down her slender body, before crouching to unfasten her suspenders and roll down the gossamer nylons.

Suddenly afraid of being overwhelmed, of losing sight of all she'd been fighting for, she began to resist fiercely. But despite her struggles her dainty bra and panties soon joined the small heap of clothes on the floor.

Lifting her in his arms, he carried her to the bed and, tossing her on to it with almost contemptuous ease, used the weight of his body to hold her there.

Realising her writhings were only inflaming him more, she forced herself to lie quite still while he ran a hand up her ribcage to cup and fondle a pink-tipped breast. Feeling the shiver that ran through her, he smiled and looked into her aquamarine eyes. What he saw there wiped the smile from his lips. 'Don't look so *scared*,' he said roughly. 'I've no intention of *hurting* you.'

She sucked air into her lungs like someone drowning. 'How can you not hurt me? You're going to take what I don't want to give.'

'Oh, Annis... Annis...' He sounded like a soul in torment. '*Why* must you keep fighting me? You could make me the happiest man in the world if only you'd——'

'I don't *want* to make you happy,' she hissed at him. 'I married you with the intention of making you as unhappy as possible.'

She heard the slight whistle of indrawn breath through his teeth. 'I wish to God I'd never used blackmail. It's only made you hate me...'

'It isn't just the blackmail. I hated you right from the start.'

Clearly shaken by her vehemence, he said slowly, 'I had hoped to overcome your initial dislike and distrust. I tried to tell myself that you couldn't really *hate* a man you didn't know, without cause...'

'I had cause enough.'

Perplexed, he half shook his head. 'You're not making any sense... What in heaven's name had you got against me?' When she stayed dumb, running out of patience he demanded angrily, 'Or is this some rubbish you've just dreamt up in order to keep me at arm's length? Well, if it is, it won't work. This time I'm——'

'No, it isn't...' she broke in desperately. 'I've always hated you because of Maya.'

Looking startled, he swung his feet to the floor and sat on the edge of the bed, facing her. 'Who told you about Maya?'

Though she was well aware it was stupid, aware she was being totally illogical, she had *wanted* to believe she'd made some dreadful mistake. *Wanted* him to deny all knowledge of Maya.

As soon as his weight lifted from her she struggled into a sitting position, pulling the clothes up to cover her nakedness. 'No one told me.'

'Then how do you know? *What* do you know?'

'Quite a lot, as it happens.'

'Well, you'd better forget it.' His voice was harsh, uncompromising. 'There's no point in causing unhappiness. Dragging up the past.'

'I'd expect you to say that,' Annis said contemptuously. 'You'd hardly want the world to know what an utter swine you are.'

For a split-second he appeared taken aback, then a shutter slid down, successfully hiding what he was thinking, feeling.

After a brief pause, he remarked carefully, 'A moment ago you said you knew quite a lot about Maya... What exactly *do* you know? Or *think* you know.'

The accusing words spilled out. 'I know you and she were lovers. I know that when you got tired of her you quite callously ditched her. I know you ruined her life and caused her death...'

His face bleak as winter, he said, 'I'm not sure how you begin to justify all these wild accusations, but I——'

'They are *not* wild accusations!'

'How else would you describe charges that haven't a word of truth in them?'

'I don't know how you have the gall to sit there and say that!' she cried passionately. 'You're as guilty as hell and you know it, even if you won't admit it.'

'Well, at least this tirade should help clear the air,' he said grimly. 'Now I know what you've been holding against me...why you've looked at me with such animosity... Listen, Annis——' he caught and held both her hands in a strong grip '—and believe me when I tell you that you've got it all wrong. I did know Maya. But I was *never* her lover. I swear it.'

Tearing her hands free, she cried, 'If you swore it on a stack of Bibles I wouldn't believe you.'

His jaw tightened and a white line appeared round his lips. 'In that case there's nothing more to be said.'

'There's a great deal more,' she countered furiously. 'For a start you could say you're sorry for what happened.'

'I'm certainly that. If I could have changed anything, made her see things in a more balanced way, I would. But Maya was a sick woman, emotionally unstable...'

Though in her heart Annis knew it was a fair assessment, she choked, 'You swine!'

'If you'd ever known Maya, you'd know it was the truth.'

'I did know her.'

Unconvinced, he pressed, 'How well?'

'Very well. She was my mother.'

He looked first shocked, then incredulous. 'What utter nonsense! Her name was Moncrief, and she couldn't have been more than thirty-two or -three at the most.'

'Moncrief was her stage name and she was thirty-nine when she died,' Annis said baldly, and saw that she had succeeded in flooring him completely.

Watching him struggle to regain his equilibrium she felt the same sense of triumph that David must have felt on toppling Goliath.

It didn't last long.

Within seconds he had recovered his self-possession and was once more master of himself and the situation.

Olive skin stretched taut over strong bones, the planes and angles of his face thrown into sharp relief, his clear-cut mouth a thin slit, he looked formidable. Curtly, he said, 'If you knew her that well, suppose you tell me the rest.'

He wasn't touching her, but there was a look in his tawny eyes that made Annis feel as though she'd been backed into a corner with his hand at her throat.

Mingling with her righteous anger came uncertainty and apprehension. 'The rest?' she faltered.

'How come she never mentioned having a family? What makes you so sure we were lovers? Why you blame me for her death... *Everything*, Annis.'

When she hesitated, reluctant, even after three long years, to talk about the past, he said with a kind of raging calm, 'I intend to know, even if I have to beat it out of you.'

Scared of that latent violence, she found herself stammering a little. 'I—I'm not sure where to start.'

'You can start by telling me what made her the kind of woman she was,' Zan suggested shortly.

'I can't tell you that,' Annis said, her slanting aquamarine eyes flickering away from the steely purpose in his. 'All I know is she was special. Amoral rather than immoral... exquisite, highly strung, magical, restless... always searching for the kind of love that, despite her beauty, she never managed to find...' Her voice wavered and she stopped speaking abruptly.

'Go on,' he ordered, no sign of softening in his hard face. 'And start from the beginning.'

After taking a moment to gather herself, she obeyed, her voice as steady and dispassionate as she could make it.

'My father was a gentle, serious man, a university professor. He was almost thirty-six, and seemed to be a confirmed bachelor, when he met Maya.

'She was just sixteen and breathtakingly beautiful even then. He lost his head completely and within a week had asked her adoptive parents' permission to marry her.

'From the age of fourteen she'd been difficult to control and, at their wits' end, they were only too pleased to give their consent. I don't think they'd ever really understood her, and as she reached adolescence they weren't able to cope with her mercurial temperament and all the problems her beauty caused...'

With a sigh, Annis continued, 'Though Dad was a nice-looking man, to Maya he must have seemed middle-aged and staid, and I still don't understand why she accepted him. Perhaps, never having got on well with her parents, she needed a father-figure. Or maybe she just wanted to get away from home...

'Whatever her reasons, she said yes, and they were married as soon as the banns could be read.

'Dad rented a picturesque old cottage on the outskirts of Rowley Beck, a small market town in Kent, and they went to live there. Ten months later I arrived, and Richard was born the following year.

'Maya was like a little girl playing with her dolls, until the novelty wore off, then she began to hate the quiet life they led at Hamble Cottage and resent being tied. Though it was a financial strain, Dad engaged a house-keeper-cum-nanny to give her more freedom. But she wanted bright lights and excitement, and there wasn't a lot of either in Rowley Beck, so she took to going up to town every day...

'Soon she was staying away nights, then weeks at a time. Dad did his best to keep her at home, but it was like trying to keep a butterfly in a cage. After a while she moved in with a stage writer-producer who bought her a sports car and promised to make her a star...'

Zan was sitting quite still, watching Annis's face through narrowed eyes.

'Though she didn't stay with him long, he kept his promise. She had talent as well as looks, and in an incredibly short time she was appearing in the West End.

'Young as we were, she insisted on us calling her Maya, rather than Mother. But though she changed her name to Moncrief and hid the fact that she had a family, she still came home periodically to make a fuss of us and bring us lavish presents.

'She was like a beautiful princess in a fairy story, and we adored her. But she always went away again...' Annis blinked, and twin tears escaped and rolled slowly down her cheeks.

Zan muttered something under his breath. Getting up abruptly he pulled on a short robe and went to stand by the window, his back to the room.

After a moment, he said gruffly, 'That kind of on-off relationship is hard for any child to take. And surely your father must have been angry and bitter?'

Staring at his broad shoulders, noting abstractedly how the silky black hair curled into the nape of his neck, she said with an odd mixture of pride and sadness, 'Dad never blamed her, nor did he stop caring about her. She knew that, and she always came home if she needed comfort or reassurance, and Dad always gave it to her. He was her rock.

'For years she burnt the candle at both ends, working hard, playing hard, living life to the full and at a pace that would have killed most people. Then, one after the other, two of the shows she was starring in flopped badly. She quarrelled with her agent, and because she'd started drinking too much no one else would take her on...' Annis's voice wavered and stopped.

Head bent, she stared blindly at her interlaced fingers until she'd regained control. Then she went on, 'Living on her own after the break-up of her last relationship, she was lonely, hard up, afraid of getting old, terrified of losing her looks, at her most vulnerable...

'Knowing she was having a struggle to pay the rent of her flat, Dad begged her to come home, and just when it seemed she might she met you and you became her new lover.'

Turning a bleak face towards her, Zan asked, curtly, 'Did she usually name the men she went to bed with?'

'No.'

'Then how did you know who her new lover was?'

'At the time I didn't. I only found out later.'

'Go on.' His voice was brittle as frosty glass.

'It was soon clear that this relationship was different. She visited us briefly and it was wonderful to see her so vital and alive, so incandescent with you.

'For the first time in her life she really *cared* and we hoped she'd finally found the love she'd been looking for.'

Swallowing past what felt like jagged shards of red-hot glass lodged in her throat, Annis forced herself to go on. 'The next time Maya came to Hamble Cottage I was the only one there. Richard was still at university, and Dad had gone to the States to undertake an extensive lecture tour.

'The change in her was heart-rending. She was gaunt and hollow-eyed, drinking heavily again and chain-smoking, clearly living on her nerves.

'When I asked her what was wrong, she said her lover wanted to end the affair and she couldn't go on without him. She was so upset and agitated that I pleaded with her not to drive back to town, but she said she *had* to, she was having dinner with him that evening and hoping to get him to change his mind. Afraid for her safety, I decided to drive her back myself and then come home by train. I left her at her flat in Knightsbridge and went to get a meal at a quiet little restaurant close to Victoria.

'I'd paid my bill and was about to leave when, by one of those strange coincidences that *do* happen, Maya walked in followed by a tall, broad-shouldered man with black curly hair. He turned his head and for a moment appeared to look straight at me...'

Some strong emotion flitted across Zan's face, and the hands hanging loosely by his sides clenched into fists.

'It was you.' There was no possibility of a mistake. That dark, arrogant, handsome face, the well-shaped head of shorn black curls, those incredible tawny eyes, had been branded indelibly on her mind ever since.

He made no attempt to deny the fact, merely stood there as though turned to granite.

Raggedly, she went on, 'Maya didn't notice me, and I escaped as quickly as I could. It was three weeks before I saw her again. She arrived very late one night, and in such a state it was a miracle she hadn't had an accident on the way. She wanted to talk, but she'd been drinking, and half the time she was barely coherent.

'I gathered that everything was over between you, and that you'd left for California that evening. For the first time she called you by name...*Zan*... It's not a common name...'

Even then Annis found herself clinging desperately to the hope that he might have *something* to say that would mitigate his part in the tragedy.

But, sounding suddenly weary, sick to death, all he said was, 'Go on, tell me the rest.'

'There's not much more to tell...'

He came back to sit on the edge of the bed, much too close, waiting, sparing her nothing.

She bit her inner lip until the blood trickled warm and salty, before continuing, 'Eventually I managed to put her to bed. It was almost dawn. When I got up to go to work she was sleeping like a log. I thought if I went home at lunch time it would be safe to leave her...

'I had a job with the local solicitor. Just before twelve o'clock the police called at the office. There'd been a blaze at Hamble Cottage, they said. The thatched roof had caught and the place had been gutted. Firemen had brought out the body of a woman...'

To keep control, Annis had been speaking in short, staccato sentences. Now, in spite of all her efforts, her voice faltered, and it was a moment or two before she could go on. 'I got in touch with Dad and he came home as soon as he could...except that we no longer had a home.

'The university were very kind and offered us temporary accommodation until we had time to sort things out. But Dad seemed to have no will left. He admitted that all he could do was think of Maya.

'When the post-mortem results came through they showed it wasn't the fire that had killed her. She'd died of a massive overdose of drugs... They believe she was smoking a cigarette when she lost consciousness...

'Dad became so quiet and withdrawn I thought he was blaming me for leaving her, and the lord knows I felt guilty enough. But in the note he left he said he couldn't forgive himself for not being there when she'd needed him.'

'The note he left?' Zan echoed, a razor-sharp edge to his voice.

'Her funeral was on the Thursday. That same night Dad drove his car into the concrete pier of a road bridge. I don't think he thought of it as suicide, just the end. He had nothing left to live for.'

'Dear God,' Zan muttered hoarsely. Adding almost to himself, 'Love's the very devil.'

Then suddenly Annis was weeping helplessly. Weeping for Maya—for a blind fool who, in her search for love, had thrown away the real thing for a handful of worthless dreams. Weeping for her father—for a love so strong and unselfish and enduring it had lasted a lifetime. Weeping for herself—for a love that might have been...

Not wanting this cold, remorseless man to witness her grief, she covered her face with her hands. But she was unable to stem the flow of tears, and they trickled between her fingers and ran down her wrists.

'Don't,' he said, but the concern in his voice only made her tears flow faster.

With an incoherent murmur, her drew her close. At first she was stiff in his arms, then she began to shake. His cheek pressed against her hair, he held her tightly, one hand stroking slowly up and down her spine, soothing the shudders that shook her.

Since the double tragedy she hadn't shed a single tear but, frozen in despair, had entombed herself behind walls of ice. Being forced to talk about it had made the first cracks appear, and now the warmth of his unexpected comfort was crumbling and melting that ice.

Her arms went around his neck and, her face buried against his throat, she began to sob, great gasping sobs that hurt her chest and took more breath than she'd got.

Still he held her, rocking her like a baby until the sobs died away and she fell to weeping quietly once more. When she was all cried out, he pulled a folded handkerchief from his pocket and mopped her up.

Sniffing, she took the hankie from his hand and blew her nose. 'I must look an absolute mess,' she said with pathetic dignity.

He studied the ravaged face, the pink nose and swollen eyes, the pale silky hair that tumbled over her bare shoulders and breasts, and contradicted softly, 'You've never looked more beautiful.'

She made a little hiccuping sound that was halfway between a laugh and a sob, and all at once began to shiver.

Stripping off his robe, he put it around her.

It still held the warmth from his body, and she could smell the clean, masculine scent of his skin.

'I'm sorry, Annis,' he apologised abruptly. 'I should never have put you through that. But I *needed* to know.'

Briefly she pressed her hands over her eyes. 'Perhaps it was like lancing a festering wound—painful but necessary to get rid of all the grief and bitterness and guilt.'

'Have you got rid of it all?'

'I don't know,' she admitted honestly. 'I still feel some guilt, and perhaps I'll always grieve for her. But I suddenly realised that I can't blame you for not loving her. No one can love—or stop loving for that matter—to order. I just wish you hadn't been...'

'Her lover?'

She nodded.

Speaking clearly, decisively, he said, 'Whether you believe me or not, I *wasn't* her lover.'

There was a ring of veracity in his voice that almost convinced her. Or was it simply that she *wanted* to be convinced?

'But it was *you* with her that night,' it was a statement not a question, '*you* she was involved with.'

He hesitated momentarily, as if considering a denial, then answered with a sigh, 'Yes, it was. And I'm partly to blame for what happened. I knew she was highly strung, living on her nerves. I should have stayed while she needed me rather than going to the States when I did.

'When I got back weeks later and heard of her death I felt guilty as hell. To some extent I still do, and believe me if I *could* alter what happened I *would*. But it was on the cards, and I don't believe I, or anyone else for that matter, could have averted the tragedy. At least not for any length of time.'

'If only she'd come home when Dad wanted her to,' Annis mourned.

'Suppose she had? How long do you think she'd have stood it there? Use your common sense, Annis. Would she have settled happily in Rowley Beck after the kind of life she'd been leading? You know damned well she wouldn't. She'd soon have got tired of being stuck in the house on her own day after day...'

'But if I'd stayed at home with her and——'

Taking her upper arms in a grip that hurt, he shook her hard. 'You'll never be free of her, never able to live your own life without guilt and regrets, until you see her as she really was. Even if she couldn't *help* being as she was, that kind of woman destroys not only herself but everyone who cares about her.'

'How can you say that?'

'How can you keep blinding yourself to the truth? The only way to master the future is to understand, and come to terms with, the past.' Bitterly he went on, 'When we first met, you tried to tell me some man was responsible for turning you into a Snow Queen. But it wasn't a man...'

'It was,' she cried a little wildly. 'It was *you*. I couldn't forget the way you'd treated Maya.'

'No, Annis, it wasn't me,' he contradicted quietly. '*She* was the one who caused you to put all your natural feelings into deep freeze. Perhaps subconsciously you were frightened of turning out like her, frightened of becoming a victim of your own emotions...'

She shook her head, refusing to listen.

'Then that night in San Francisco you forgot those repression and inhibitions. Next day when you realised that you'd behaved like a warm, passionate woman, it scared the living daylights out of you. That was why you were so afraid of repeating your "mistake". Why you're still afraid.'

'No, it isn't that.'

His hands loosened their grip and slid beneath the robe to stroke the warmth of her back and draw her closer. 'In that case, what is it?'

When she failed to answer, he tilted her face up to his. 'Don't try to pretend you don't want me. Even though you've done your best to resist it, there's been an overwhelming attraction between us from the start... Hasn't there, Annis?' he pressed.

'Yes,' she admitted huskily, and fancied she heard his sigh of relief.

Those extraordinary cat-green eyes searched her face. 'Then tell me why you're fighting so hard against it. Is it solely because I was involved with Maya?'

She nodded mutely.

He pounced. 'But you knew about that in San Francisco and it didn't prevent you sleeping with me.'

Then she hadn't been thinking, only feeling.

Colour came into her pale face. 'That's one of the reasons I regretted it. I felt as though I'd betrayed her.'

'Do you still feel that way? Still believe I was her lover?'

'I don't *want* to believe it.'

The gleam of triumph in his eyes stiffened her resolution. When he bent to touch his mouth to hers she somehow found the strength to turn her face away. 'No, I don't want you to kiss me. I don't want to...'

But she couldn't tell him she was afraid of getting any more involved, afraid of loving him. Scared of being used and then thrown aside when his infatuation had burnt itself out.

'...I—I don't want a sexual relationship with you or anyone,' she finished desperately.

'Do you intend to cut yourself off from the warmth of all human relationships? Spend the rest of your life alone, afraid to feel, afraid to love, afraid to be a woman?'

Did she? The only man she'd ever wanted was right here with her. Was she going to let the traumas of the past, or fear of the future, spoil what she could have? Leave her with the kind of cold, barren existence Zan had just pictured?

So what if he did end the affair when he became tired of her? She would know what it was like to be wanted, to share passion and a kind of caring. At least she would have memories to warm herself with.

She had nothing to lose; she'd already lost it. She couldn't be indifferent to him, and she could no longer hate him. There was no way of stepping back over that line.

Yet was she brave enough to step forward? To chance falling even deeper in love with him? Passion, though flaming hot and fiery, was relatively easy to control. It was love, as Zan had said, that was the very devil. To love was to give oneself as a hostage to fortune. She could end up alone and desolate, utterly destroyed.

Like Maya.

But if she could be strong enough to control her feelings for him, to live with him without losing her head, her heart, or her soul, she might come out of it relatively unscathed...

As she sat, blonde head bent, staring blindly at the indigo bedspread, he jumped to his feet with a growl of anger and frustration and headed for the door. His hand was on the latch when she whispered, 'Zan...'

He paused. His smooth, bronzed back gleamed in the light and she could see the tension in those broad shoulders. Stiffly he turned his dark head to look at her.

The aquamarine eyes were bright with tears. 'Please don't go.'

CHAPTER NINE

HIS voice soft and dangerous, Zan said, 'Don't play games with me, Annis. I refuse to tolerate any more of this blow hot, blow cold treatment. If I stay I won't allow you to change your mind again tomorrow. I intend to be the one who dictates when it ends. So if you want me on those terms...'

'I do.' She held out her arms.

When he went into them she cradled his dark head against her breast and, already anticipating the day when he would send her away, she died a little.

He seemed to know. When he made love to her there was no fine, careless rapture, but rather a passionate intensity, an added poignancy, as though he too was acknowledging that their relationship was to be brief. A temporary thing.

Afterwards she cried—not knowing quite why—and he held her against his heart with a tenderness that could have been mistaken for love.

Next morning when she opened her eyes she found him leaning over her, propped on one elbow. He was studying her face with an intensity that suggested he wanted to memorise every minute detail.

She smiled at him a little uncertainly.

He smiled back and kissed her, but the happiness that had been so apparent in his face that morning in San Francisco was unaccountably missing.

With their added closeness had come a deeper perception, a kind of sixth sense, and she felt sure that he too was regretting the past and fearing the future.

Though what had he to fear when the power to order the future lay in his own hands?

As though he didn't want her to decipher his expression he smiled again, banishing that troubled look, and asked lightly, 'How about a champagne breakfast in bed?'

She made an effort to respond to his deliberate change of mood. 'It sounds marvellously decadent. Unless of course I'm the one who has to get it,' she finished mischievously.

He pretended to consider the matter, then offered, 'I'll get it if you agree to make it worth my while.'

'I might have known there'd be strings attached.'

'Just a kiss or two.'

'Oh, is that all?' She looked disappointed.

His mouth quirked. 'Were you expecting more?'

'Much more.'

'Such as what?'

'I wouldn't want to put ideas into your head,' she said demurely.

He gave her a smouldering look. 'Believe me, I'm not short of ideas. For instance you could...' Putting his lips to her ear he whispered a few words, and laughed when she blushed rosily.

Some time later, lying quietly in the crook of his arm, she admitted that as far as loving him was concerned she was fighting a losing battle. Already she belonged more to him than to herself.

He was, and perhaps had always been, her master. First he'd controlled her with threats, now it was with the strength of his passion—and the answering passion he roused in her.

She ought to despise herself for letting it happen so swiftly and completely, but all she could feel was a kind of awe at the intensity of her feelings.

Staring up at the white, sun-dappled ceiling, she wondered if Maya had felt that kind of spiritual as well as bodily ecstasy.

Damn! Damn! She hadn't meant to doubt him, to let the thought of Maya and the past intrude.

Seeing the fleeting frown that pleated her smooth forehead, he asked, 'Why the frown?'

'I was just wondering what that could be,' she said mendaciously.

'What?'

She pointed. 'There's a little black spot on the ceiling.'

'So there is.' He sounded fascinated.

'What do you think it is?'

'A fly?' he hazarded.

'It isn't moving.'

'So it's a lazy fly.'

'Speaking of laziness——' she elbowed him in the ribs and heard his little grunt of surprise '—you said we'd have breakfast in bed.'

'Sassy, eh?' Rolling over, he caught her wrists and pinned her hands above her head. 'Now who's feeling impudent?'

'Not me,' she denied hurriedly. 'I just thought you might be getting hungry.'

'I am.' But his eyes were lingering on her—on her long, slender throat and her creamy, pink-tipped breasts.

'And you promised me champagne,' she reminded him breathlessly, as his mouth hovered with intent.

'Well, as I make a point of always keeping my promises...' He sighed and released her wrists, but not before he'd used his lips and teeth and tongue to make her gasp and squirm deliciously.

By the time he brought back a try loaded with warm flaky croissants and iced champagne, her heartbeat had returned to normal and she was able to meet his mocking glance with comparative composure.

Any hint of sadness or insecurity put aside, the next couple of weeks were full of the kind of jewel-bright happiness that came only rarely.

As though catching their mood, the weather had turned glorious. After spending a short time each morning in the office, Zan insisted on making the most of it. Their daylight hours were used for country walks and picnics, trips down the Thames and excursions to the seaside, while their nights were filled with lovemaking.

On the surface it was complete and satisfying, but beneath the euphoria lay a driving hunger that was never really appeased.

Zan made love to her with a strange urgency, an exquisite passion, which she met and matched with a bittersweet passion of her own.

On both their parts was a kind of desperation to enjoy to the full what they had, while it was within their grasp.

One Friday evening, as they were returning from a day spent at Kew Gardens, Mrs Matheson met them in the hall to say, 'Mrs Warrener rang. I told her you were gallivanting again.'

Zan grinned unrepentantly. 'You sound disapproving.'

Mary sniffed. 'She asked me to remind you that they're expecting you to dine at Rydal Lodge tonight. Seven-thirty for eight . . .'

Zan glanced at his watch, then dropping an arm around Annis's shoulders, said, 'We've just nice time to shower and change.'

In their bedroom, with the gleam in his green-gold eyes that always took her breath away, he asked enticingly, 'Shower with me?'

'Only if you promise to behave yourself,' she said primly, rummaging for clean undies.

He shuddered. 'You sound just like Mary...'

'How long has she been with you?'

'About twelve years. I engaged her as soon as I could afford a housekeeper. My younger brothers and sisters were still at home and they needed someone to look after them.'

'Where did you live then?'

'In an old, damp house in Battersea that would have frightened off most women. But thank God Mary was made of sterner stuff.'

'Has she been widowed long?'

'Her husband had just died and she was thinking of going to live with her sister when I offered her a job... Now, are you ready for that shower, or do you want to carry on discussing our housekeeper?'

Warming to the *our*, she nevertheless protested, 'I just find her interesting.'

He leered at her. 'I could make a shower a great deal more interesting. But as you look tired, I promise that all I'll do is dry you.'

She glanced at him from beneath long lashes, and relenting, said, 'I'm not *that* tired.'

'Hallelujah,' he murmured piously.

Later, warm and dry and scented, she thanked heaven that though he might not love her it was abundantly clear he still wanted her.

Often, at the back of her mind, was the thought that his obsession might soon be over, his passion for her burning itself out in one of those fiery nights of lovemaking.

It was five weeks now since he'd first made love to her. Five weeks since that night in San Francisco...

Five weeks...

The realisation was suddenly branded into her consciousness, along with the fact that for the past few days she'd felt a little queasy...

She'd put the slight upset down to some prawns that hadn't seemed quite fresh, but now the suspicion that it could have had a different cause grew in her mind...

The warmth that filled her at the thought that she might be carrying Zan's baby was almost instantly replaced by fear and apprehension. What would *his* reaction be? Their bargain tied her to him for at least a year, so he was bound to find out. Perhaps he would be angry? Try to make her get rid of it?

Well, she wouldn't. *Nothing* would induce her to do such a thing. But almost immediately, remembering the way he'd struggled to keep his own family intact, she realised she was doing him a grave injustice. Even so, a great anxiety remained.

After her own insecure childhood, if she *did* have a baby she wanted it to be born into a happy home, to enjoy the stability of a lasting marriage, to have parents who loved each other and stayed together. Not be the outcome of a strange, passionate relationship that was almost certainly doomed to end in misery and heartbreak.

Making a determined effort, she tried to fight down the disquiet and look on the bright side. There could be other reasons for her being late. She mustn't jump to conclusions, or allow herself to keep worrying about it.

But that was easier said than done.

The spell of fine weather appeared to be coming to an end, and a fine mist was descending as Zan drove the BMW through London's early evening traffic to Rydal Lodge.

They were met at the door with a hearty welcome. Richard hugged his sister warmly, then the two men shook hands.

When Linda had kissed Annis, a little in awe of Zan even now, she hesitated.

He pulled a doleful face. 'Don't I get a kiss?'

Laughing, she obliged, before leading the way inside, saying over her shoulder, 'How lovely to see you both. Mrs Matheson says you've spent the last two weeks gallivanting, so tell me everything you've been doing...'

Zan gave Annis the smiling sidelong glance that never failed to quicken her pulses, before raising a dark brow at Linda and asking, '*Everything*?'

As the colour washed into Annis's cheeks, her sister-in-law laughed and went pink in her turn. 'Well, perhaps not *everything*...'

The time passed quickly and the evening, which Annis had had reservations about, proved to be such a success that it was quite late before they got up to go.

Having said their thanks and goodbyes they were on the point of leaving, when Richard exclaimed, 'Oh I almost forgot. It's amazing what turns up when you're moving house...'

Going to the bureau, he opened a drawer and pulled out an envelope. 'I wondered if you'd like to have these? Maya sent them to me a month or so before she died.'

A shade hesitantly, he added, 'It just struck me that with the fire and everything you might not have a photograph of her, and I've got several... Oh, and there's this.' He produced a letter with a US stamp. 'Sheila said it had been sent to your office.'

Aware that by her side Zan had stiffened, and feeling as though she herself had just walked into a brick wall, Annis took the envelopes from her brother and, mumbling her thanks, stuffed them into her bag as she made her way across the hall.

'You'll come again before too long, won't you?' Linda asked eagerly.

It was Zan who answered, with what sounded like genuine enthusiasm, 'We'd be delighted to. But you must have a meal with us first.'

At the door, they discovered it had turned quite foggy, and as the BMW slid down the drive, its headlights searched the wall of mist like the moving antennae of some animal.

Perhaps it was the impression of greyness pressing in on all sides that added to Annis's feeling of being imprisoned.

She glanced uneasily at Zan, only to find he had discarded his social mask and his dark face, earlier alive and expressive, was now aloof and shuttered, the face of a gaoler.

A shiver running through her, she told herself not to be a fool. Still the sensation of being trapped persisted unnervingly.

They got back to Griffin House to find Mrs Matheson had obviously retired for the night and, apart from the twin carriage-lamps that glowed through the mist, the place was in darkness.

'I'll think I'll go straight up to bed,' Annis said hurriedly.

But when she attempted to make a beeline for the stairs, Zan's fingers closed around her wrist like a steel shackle, stopping her in her tracks. 'Don't go yet. I want to talk to you.'

What about? she wondered anxiously. The things that Richard had given her? Or had he noticed she wasn't herself and, with that sixth sense he so often displayed where she was concerned, picked up her own uneasy suspicion that she might be pregnant?

Feeling unable to cope with any kind of confrontation that night, she objected, 'Surely it can wait until morning?' and was angry with herself for sounding nervous.

'No, it can't wait until morning.' A hand in the small of her back he propelled her towards the kitchen.

Quivers of apprehension running through her, she protested weakly, 'I'm tired.'

Dark and dominating, he would have none of it. 'You can stay in bed all day tomorrow if you wish.'

Knowing it was useless trying to fight such arrogant determination, she sank down in the nearest armchair. Then wished she hadn't when he touched a switch and she found herself sitting—like some suspect about to be questioned—in a pool of light cast by the standard lamp.

The room was still warm, the remains of a fire glowing in the grate. But as though declaring his intention of making the interrogation a lengthy one, Zan stirred the embers into life and, crouching on his haunches, constructed a pyramid of split logs.

Annis found herself watching his hands. He had interesting hands, long and lean and mobile, beautifully shaped and sensitive, despite their strength.

Glancing over his shoulder, he asked in a voice that was used to giving orders, used to being obeyed, 'Aren't you going to look at your letter?'

So it was the letter.

With a feeling of reprieve on one front and anxiety on the other, she took out the envelope addressed in Stephen's untidy fist, and tore it open.

Having skimmed through the pages, she breathed a sigh of relief, and began to feel slightly less guilty about her part in turning his life upside down.

More than a little stilted, as if written by someone who *wanted* to sound like a troubleshooter but was still finding it difficult to fit the image, to see himself in such colourful and romantic terms, it was innocuous and cheerful enough.

Though so far he'd been no further afield than California and its neighbouring states, he told her, his new job was an interesting challenge which he was enjoying immensely. He liked the mild climate and the sunshine, got on well with his American colleagues, and was pleased with the condominium the firm had found for him.

Only towards the end did he become slightly maudlin, the real man showing through. 'If you were here with me,' he'd written, 'things would be perfect. You're the only woman I've ever loved, and I miss you a lot...'

But the declaration seemed curiously passionless, and she had the feeling that he was almost enjoying the pangs of unrequited love.

Looking up at Zan, who had risen to his feet and was leaning against the mantel, Annis found his tawny eyes fixed on her with a bleak, dissecting look.

Silently she held out the letter.

He shook his head, his mouth indenting with wry self-mockery. 'I've never considered a husband has a right to read his wife's mail.'

'Neither have I, unless he's given that privilege,' she answered coolly. 'However, I would like you to read this.'

Taking it from her he scanned it rapidly, then glancing up, commented sardonically, 'It doesn't exactly burn the paper it's written on.'

'No...' After a moment she added with a touch of irony, 'So if you're quite satisfied, perhaps I could go to bed now?'

His beautiful mouth tightened ominously, and she knew she'd succeeded in aggravating him.

'Don't you have something else to look at?' His curt query jolted her.

With a feeling of reluctance that amounted almost to foreboding, Annis took out the second envelope. Inside a single folded sheet of monogrammed notepaper were two snapshots of Maya. They appeared to have been taken outside an old coaching inn, and in each of them she was smiling brilliantly.

The note, dated a couple of months before her death, had clearly been written when she was still on top of the world. It was completely self-orientated, as always, the flamboyant style contrasting oddly with the small, cramped handwriting.

'My own darling Ricky, I can't begin to tell you how ecstatically happy I am! At last I've found the man of my dreams. He's as dark and handsome as Lucifer, and the most wonderful lover any woman could wish for. Perhaps I shouldn't confess a thing like that to my own son, but you're a big boy now. We've just spent a heavenly weekend in the Cotswolds—that's where the photos were taken. The stumbling-block is his...' The next word was heavily scored out, then the letter went on, 'But in the circumstances I must be discreet. We are both newsworthy—he's a top businessman—and if the media got wind of our affair they'd have a field day. However, when he's dealt with some personal problems we can be together openly and for always. I can hardly wait. My fondest love, as ever. Maya.'

Knowing now that Zan had lied to her, Annis sat still and silent, gazing down at the damning words, feeling as though she'd been turned to stone.

'Am I to be granted the same privilege?'

Zan's question brought her smooth, silvery blonde head up. For a moment she stared at him blindly, then anger, bitter as Dead Sea apples on her tongue, she said, 'Yes, I think you *should* read it... Now if you'll excuse me.'

But as she made an attempt to rise, his hand shot out and fastened on her shoulder. 'Don't go.' Without hurting her, he applied enough downward pressure to make it difficult to disobey him. 'We still need to talk.'

When she sank back, he transferred his attention to the note. As he read it, his tawny eyes seemed to blaze in the frozen mask of his face. Then with an angry exclamation, he crumpled it into a ball and threw it into the flames.

'Burning the evidence?' Annis asked scornfully.

Controlling himself with an effort, he said flatly, 'I only wish Richard had burnt that rubbish straight away instead of coming up with it just when things seemed to be working out.'

'You call it rubbish, but it was the truth, wasn't it?'

Bending, he caught hold of both her hands, his grip painful. 'I want you to try and put it right out of your mind.'

'*Wasn't it*?' she insisted.

'There was *some* truth in it,' he admitted heavily. 'But for everyone's sake, you *have* to make an effort to forget it.'

Ignoring his words, she tried to pull her hands free, saying through stiff lips, 'You're hurting me.'

'I'm sorry.' He released his grip. 'I didn't mean to. But reading that blasted note made me feel so furious.'

'But not *guilty*?' Lifting her chin she stared at him, making no effort to hide the cold contempt.

'Don't look at me like that.' Taking her shoulders, he shook her. 'I won't allow you to spoil what we've got. What's happened in the past shouldn't make any difference to us. You're mine now, a warm, passionate woman... Nothing's changed.'

'Everything's changed. I can't stay with you knowing how you lied to me.'

His face grew pale beneath the tan. 'No matter what that letter seems to suggest, I didn't lie to you...'

'I don't believe you,' she cried.

'Listen to me, Annis——' he gave her a little shake to emphasise each word '—I was *never* Maya's lover. But as it's not possible to prove, you'll just have to take my word and trust me.'

She shook her head. 'I'm leaving.'

Softly, dangerously, he said, 'I won't let you go.'

'You can't stop me.'

His hands dropped to his sides as though discounting physical restraint, before he responded with quiet certainty, 'Oh, yes, I can...'

'I noticed you didn't finish your sherry tonight, nor your wine, and you scarcely ate a thing...'

His quiet statement made her heartbeat falter then start racing. 'I—I had a headache,' she stammered.

'Was it the headache that made you look so *distraite* and kept you unusually quiet all evening?'

'Yes, it was,' she declared boldly.

'That's a pity.' His voice was smooth, solicitous. 'I rather thought you might have some good news for me...'

Watching all the colour drain from her face he said, 'In some ways we're so close that I quite often know what's going through your mind.' When she said nothing, he continued, 'If you *are* having a baby, it happened that very first night in San Francisco...

'After learning about Maya and realising there were even more problems than I'd envisaged, I made sure you wouldn't get pregnant—at least until those problems had been put behind us. Now it seems my precautions may have come too late...'

'Not necessarily.' Flushing a little, she went on, 'I've never been very regular. It might be a false alarm . . .'

'And it might not.'

'Either way I refuse to stay with you.'

Furiously, he began, 'If you hadn't read that damned note——'

'But I *have* read it.'

'Well, if you think I'm going to let the outpourings of a neurotic woman ruin both our lives you're quite wrong. You're staying and——'

'You can't *make* me stay.' Desperately, she added, 'I'd sooner tell Linda and Richard the truth.'

After a taut silence, he asked, 'If there *is* a baby, do you want to keep it?'

'Of course I want to keep it,' she cried, and saw some of his tautness relax. She gazed up at him white-faced and vulnerable, her clear, aquamarine eyes mirroring her distress.

'Then if you stop to think about it, Annis, I'm sure you'll see that to stay with me is by far the wisest course. Sexually we're compatible, to say the least. We like the same things, and enjoy each other's company. Surely we've enough going for us to build a future together?'

The thing she'd always known—that because he didn't *love* her their relationship was bound to be a temporary one—surfaced. 'For how long?' she asked bitterly. 'As long as your obsession lasts? And then what—a quick divorce?'

'I don't believe in divorce. I'm offering you a lifetime's commitment.'

Despite everything, for a moment she was dreadfully tempted to try and grasp that dream of happiness. But common sense told her it *was* just a dream. She shook her head. 'It would never work.'

'We can *make* it work. With give and take on both sides we can have a good and lasting relationship.'

'Based on what?'

After hesitating briefly, he answered, 'On mutual liking and respect.' Then he urged, 'Annis, stay with me *willingly*. I *know* we can make each other happy. Why don't you just stay with me until the child is born? Let our child be something that draws us together, and if, after the birth, you really can't bear me in your life, then you can go.'

For a moment she wavered, shaken by his apparent sincerity. Then she laughed scornfully. 'You can hardly expect us to be *happy*. As I neither like nor respect you, and could never forget you were my mother's lover, all we could make each other would be *unhappy*.'

He went white to the lips and for one awful moment she thought he was going to strike her, then he said coldly, 'Then that's how it must be. I'd rather be unhappy with you than happy with any other woman.'

After a moment she said dully, 'All right, you win. I'll stay with you. But I won't sleep with you.'

His face was a blank mask, no feelings exposed. Only his eyes were alive and they blazed with a terrible anger. Quietly, implacably, he said, 'I think you will.'

'You'll have to use force.'

'I'll do whatever's necessary. I'm determined that from now on we're having as normal a married life as possible.'

He stooped to lift her out of her chair, holding her tightly in case she struggled. But well aware that it would be useless to fight him, she lay supine in his arms as he carried her up the stairs.

In their bedroom he put her down on the bed and began to kiss and caress her, while he removed her clothes with care.

But even when his mouth was exploring hers, his hand fondling her full, warm breast, her eyes wide open, she lay like a rag doll.

It was passive resistance at its most prohibitive.

She was wondering desperately how long she could keep it up, when he lifted his mouth from hers to say softly, 'It won't work, Annis.'

He closed her eyelids with kisses, then began to caress her again with feather-light strokes that goose-pimpled her skin. His hands and mouth tantalising, tormenting, he used all his skill and patience to rouse her, gradually bringing every inch of her body to throbbing life.

He didn't speak again during that long, slow seduction of the senses, but felt a savage satisfaction at the betraying signs of quickened breathing and hardening nipples, the little gasps she couldn't control as he teased and touched them with lips and tongue.

When he finally moved over her, her arms went around his neck and her mouth opened to his with a wordless, hungry passion that matched his own.

He took her with the fierce triumph of some conqueror, enjoying to the full the little whimpers of pleasure he forced from her, before allowing his own iron control to slip and send them both tumbling into the precipice.

When his breathing slowed and his pulse-rate returned to normal, Zan rolled on to his back. Drawing Annis into his arms, he settled her head on his shoulder, before pulling the clothes over their sweat-slicked bodies.

CHAPTER TEN

ANNIS awoke next morning with a feeling of warmth and security. Safe in the crook of Zan's arm, her head on his chest, she was at home where she belonged.

As she lay, eyes closed, quietly savouring the feeling of joy and wellbeing, her mind stirred into life. In a moment her happiness had drained away like water from a sink when someone pulled the plug, and she was reproaching herself bitterly for her weakness and stupidity.

She had neither wanted nor intended to sleep with him again, but he only had to touch her to engender the most powerful feeling she'd ever known, a longing to be in his arms that obliterated all resolve, all restraint, all sense of right or wrong.

A sigh escaped her.

'Awake?' he asked, his hand beginning to fondle one of her beautiful, firm breasts.

She made a small, indistinct sound, and froze.

He knew immediately. Drawing back a little to look down at her, he said urgently, 'Don't let the past come between us, Annis. Don't keep on fighting your own feelings.'

It was no use fighting them, she knew and admitted the fact. While he still wanted her she was his for the taking. But the past would always come between them, and the inner turmoil, the conflict of loyalties, would sooner or later tear her apart.

To her chagrin, tears filled her eyes and crept beneath her lashes.

'Don't cry,' he whispered, cradling her blonde head against his chest. 'Everything's all right.'

But it wasn't.

And with that sixth sense he had where she was concerned, Zan picked up her mental withdrawal, and knew that while her body was open to him her mind was closed.

From that moment a chasm seemed to widen between them. Though they slept in the same bed, physically as close as two people could be, they no longer *communicated*. They made love with a wild, passionate intensity, but never met on any other level.

Over the next few days, like a pair of polite strangers forced to share a house, they spoke only when it was necessary, and then stiltedly, as though the dialogue had been scripted for them.

Zan went back to his office and, saying that he had a great deal to catch up on, worked all hours God sent.

When Annis—who was feeling herself again—made it clear that instead of working for him she wanted to go back to running Help, Zan let her have her way. His only stipulations were that she should stick to the administrative side and, before she actually began work, get her doctor's approval.

Annis had an appointment to see Dr Roberts the following Monday when, on a cold, wet Friday morning, she discovered that her 'pregnancy' had been a false alarm.

Zan was very late home that evening. Wondering what he'd say, she waited for him by the fire with mixed emotions.

When she finally heard his key in the lock she put down the book she'd been trying to read, and made an effort to curb her agitation.

He came through to the kitchen, one hand loosening the knot in his tie. With a touch of anxiety she saw he looked whacked, his lean face, with its chiselled planes and firm jaw, showed signs of strain. A dark stubble shadowed his cleft chin.

Evidently surprised to see her, he said shortly, 'I thought you'd be in bed.'

'There's something I wanted to talk to you about...' All day she'd been planning how best to break it to him, but now she found herself just blurting it out. 'I—I'm not having a baby after all...'

If she'd been looking at him she would have seen his face tighten with a spasm of pain that was almost anguish.

But her eyes on her clenched hands, all she was conscious of was a frigid silence.

So what had she expected? she thought bitterly. That he'd be sad? Disappointed?

She'd been both. Yet at the same time, knowing the circumstances were all wrong, relieved.

Looking up now to find his expression a stony mask, she saw he didn't care a jot. It just didn't *matter* to him. Chilled to the bone by his non-reaction, she cried, 'I wish I'd left the night I read that letter. I wish you hadn't made me stay with you...'

It seemed as though he was about to make some appeal but then, his hand dropping to his side, he agreed icily, 'So do I,' and turning on his heel, stalked out.

She sat quite still, feeling as though she'd been stabbed through the heart.

Physically they were still necessary to each other, but how could they go on living together with no other point of contact, and the past lying like a dark shadow between them?

For a long time she remained staring into the dying embers of the fire. At length, not knowing what else to do, she went upstairs.

Her whole body stiff, she moved slowly, laboriously, like someone who had been mortally wounded.

Their bedroom was empty and so was the bathroom. As soon as she'd washed her face and cleaned her teeth, she crept shivering into bed.

In spite of everything, she had wanted desperately to be near him, wanted him to hold her.

After lying awake for hours in the dark, listening to the sound of silence, she faced the fact that he wasn't going to come. All at once the tears welled up and she was weeping as though her heart would break. She cried for a long time. The first blackbird was singing a Te Deum and a grey dawn was lightening the sky before she fell into an uneasy doze.

A tap at the door aroused her. As she propped herself up on one elbow, Mrs Matheson bustled in with a tray.

If her sharp glance noted Annis's ravaged face and the fact that she'd slept alone, the housekeeper made no comment, remarking only, 'I'm away to see my sister. But as it's nearly ten I thought I'd pop up first in case you weren't feeling well.'

'I'm fine, thank you,' Annis managed. 'Just lazy.'

'Well, then, take your tea while it's hot.' Though Mary's tone was brusque her eyes were compassionate.

When the door had closed behind the Scotswoman's sturdy figure, Annis, her mouth parched, drank two cups of tea gratefully.

Then moving in what seemed to be slow motion, she showered and dressed, all the time wondering where Zan had got to. Wondering if he was all right.

The morning looked cool and overcast, and a glance out of the window showed that a light rain was falling. Feeling lost and alone, she made herself a piece of toast and was sitting huddled by the kitchen fire eating it when the bell rang.

Going reluctantly to the door, she found her visitor was Matt. Wearing a well-cut business suit, he looked taller, more serious than she'd ever seen him look.

Though his blue Mercedes was parked only yards away the fine drizzle had already settled on his shoulders and dewed his smooth, dark hair.

There was something about his handsome face, the way he was looking at her, that flustered her. 'I'm afraid Zan's out,' she faltered.

'I'm aware of that,' he said briefly. 'I've just left him.'

She felt a quick relief. 'Then he's at the office?'

'Didn't you know?'

'I wasn't sure...' Her words tailed off, and she found herself wondering what Matt was doing here when he knew Zan wasn't home.

As though reading her thoughts, he informed her, 'It was *you* I wanted to see.'

'Oh...' She stared at him, completely at a loss.

'Perhaps I could come in?'

Flushing a little, she answered, 'Of course,' and turned towards the sitting-room.

'The kitchen will do fine,' he said.

Wanting time to collect herself, she murmured, 'I'll make some coffee.'

While she busied herself with the percolator, he strolled over to the window and stood for a minute looking out over the wet garden.

A glance in his direction told her that whatever had brought him here clearly mattered. She could see the tautness in his neck and shoulders.

Turning to face her, he asked abruptly, 'What's wrong between you and Zan?'

'What makes you think there's anything wrong?'

'Have you *looked* at him lately?' Matt demanded. 'Don't you realise what you're doing to him? If he didn't love you so damn much——'

'He doesn't love me,' she broke in raggedly.

Matt laughed incredulously. 'Surely you don't believe that? The man's crazy about you... If he weren't, you wouldn't have such power to hurt him.'

Such power to hurt him... The words seemed to echo inside her head, and suddenly she recalled Zan saying bleakly, 'Love's the very devil...'

And it was! Good honest passion was relatively easy to cope with. It was love that tore one apart, that caused such torment and pain.

'Don't you think he's hurt me?' she flared.

After a critical look at her pallor, the mauve shadows beneath her eyes, the puffiness of her lids, he admitted, 'You certainly don't appear to have emerged unscathed. If it was merely a lovers' tiff... But it's more than that, isn't it?'

'I think you should ask him.'

'I just did, and he told me to mind my own bloody business.'

She lifted her chin, and meeting his gaze squarely, suggested, 'Then maybe you should do that?'

A glint of respect in his deep-set hazel eyes, he agreed, 'Maybe I should. But I owe Zan a great deal, and I've no intention of standing idly by while he's on the rack.'

As they faced each other like antagonists, he went on, 'I suppose you know he's working himself into the ground?'

'Being away so much, there was a lot to catch up on,' she muttered defensively.

Matt said a rude word under his breath. 'Do you take me for an idiot? Zan's always been able to delegate, and I've been on the spot to see that things kept running smoothly...' Then, in exasperation, 'What the hell are you *doing* to him, woman?'

So he was blaming her for everything.

She saw red. 'You should be asking what *he's* doing to *me*.'

'Right, I'm asking... And it had better be good.'

Sinking into a chair, Annis pressed her fingers to her temples for a moment, as if to help still the throbbing.

Although she wasn't looking at him, she could feel the impact of his waiting gaze right through her slender body.

Raising her head, she said, 'Oh, it's good, all right... Perhaps you don't know just how much he "helped" Linda and Richard?'

When Matt looked blank, she went on bitterly, 'As well as borrowing Mrs Sheldon, he arranged for a private nursing home for Linda, found them a house, created a better job for Richard...'

When Matt continued to look blank, she added, 'He also paid off their overdraft and all their other debts... *And he did it solely to have a hold on me*.'

Dropping into the chair opposite, Matt frowned. 'Are you trying to tell me he blackmailed you?'

'I'm not trying, I *am* telling you. He threatened to "withdraw his support" if I didn't marry him.'

'You could have called his bluff. Told him to go to hell.'

'That's easy to say,' she cried, 'but I *cared* about Linda and Richard... So, though I hated him, I dared not chance it.'

'I don't believe you hated him,' Matt told her bluntly. 'You were uneasy when he broke the news of your forthcoming marriage, but there was absolutely no doubt about the chemistry between you.'

Biting her lip, she admitted, 'Perhaps I only *wanted* to hate him. Right from the start I knew there was an almost irresistible attraction.'

Matt looked nonplussed. 'Zan must have been aware of that, so why did he feel the need to use strong-arm tactics?'

'I was fighting it. Determined not to get involved with the man I knew was responsible for destroying almost everything I cared about...'

She swallowed hard, then went on, 'You see, by some strange quirk of fate he'd been my mother's lover.'

Clearly taken aback, Matt echoed, 'Your mother's lover? Are you sure about that? Certain there's no mistake?'

Flatly, she said, 'I'd seen them together. In any case he admitted the association, though he kept denying that he and Maya had been lovers... When he ended the affair she took an overdose, and on the day of her funeral my father killed himself.'

Matt just stared at her, while every vestige of colour drained from his face, leaving him ashen.

'I *wanted* to believe he hadn't been her lover,' Annis went on bleakly, 'and I'd almost succeeded in convincing myself... Then by chance I read a letter which mentioned a weekend they'd spent together in the Cotswolds, and which made it clear that he'd lied.

'Though I've come to accept that he *wasn't* to blame for what happened to Maya—it was her own basic weakness—somehow I can't forgive him for lying to me...'

They sat like two figures of stone, the only sound and movement the rustle of a log setting in the grate.

Then Matt stirred, and said with sombre certainty, 'He wasn't lying. Maya did spend a weekend in the Cotswolds, but the man with her wasn't Zan, it was me.'

'You!'

A hard flush lying along his cheekbones, he went on doggedly, 'At that time my marriage was going through a rough patch. Helen was having a difficult pregnancy with Lisa, and had been in the hospital for weeks. Mrs Sheldon had taken the two boys to Jersey to stay with my mother, and I was on my own...'

Annis drew a deep, unsteady breath.

His eyes dark with self-loathing, Matt said grimly, 'You can't blame me any more than I blame myself.'

'How did you come to meet her?' Annis asked, her voice just above a whisper.

'We met in a restaurant, where we were both dining alone. I offered her a lift home, and she asked me to stay... I was a damned fool ever to get involved, but Maya was gay and beautiful, and I was hellish lonely.

'When Zan found out he was *livid*. By that time I'd come to my senses and was trying to end the affair. But Maya didn't want to let go. Though I'd never lied to her, she'd *presumed* a lot of things...

'That was when Zan stepped in. He coped with all the hassle, and as a matter of expediency I was transferred temporarily to AP Worldwide's set-up in Santa Clara.

'It was only when I came home for Lisa's birth that I heard Maya had died. I was sorry. In spite of everything she was oddly innocent, somehow childlike and pathetic...'

The percolator began to bubble noisily. Like someone in a dream, Annis got to her feet and reached for two mugs.

Matt stood up, shaking his head. 'Not for me. I've got to go and talk to Helen.'

'You're not...?'

'Don't you think it's about time she knew?'

'No!' Annis cried sharply. Then, more carefully, 'Why do you think Zan didn't tell me the truth...?' Without pulling any punches, she went on, 'I don't believe he was protecting *you*. He was afraid of Helen getting hurt... afraid of your marriage breaking up.'

'I'm sure you're right,' Matt admitted wryly.

With a quiet authority, she suggested, 'So for everyone's sake let's say it's over and done with, best forgotten.'

'Can *you* forget?'

'I believe I can now I know what really happened.' She looked at him with a level gaze. 'Thank you for telling me. It couldn't have been easy.'

'I could hardly do less.' He hesitated, then asked, 'This *will* put things right between you and Zan?'

'I don't know,' she admitted honestly. 'I hope so.'

At the door he turned to say, 'Try to forgive me. I'd like us to be friends.'

The latch clicked behind him and all at once Annis began to tremble. She poured herself a coffee with unsteady hands and, sipping it, thought over all she knew.

Everything fell into place like a jigsaw.

She recalled her own first impression that the man in Maya's life had been married. 'Tall, dark, and handsome', and 'a top businessman' fitted Matt just as well as Zan. And in Maya's letter the short word that had been crossed out was almost certainly 'wife', followed by the more cautious, 'When he's dealt with some personal problems...'

Gradually warmth replaced the agitation and she felt her spirits rise for the first time in days. Zan hadn't lied to her, hadn't been Maya's lover. She hugged the thought to her like some priceless gift. All he'd done was try and protect his sister's happiness...

Her thoughts were interrupted by the sound of a door closing. She jumped up eagerly as Zan walked in.

His darkly handsome face looked drawn and weary, as though he hadn't slept at all the previous night.

She wanted to run to him, to put her arms around him and hold him tight, but his air of cold aloofness kept her at bay.

As she waited, hoping for some sign of softening, he said without preamble, 'I've decided to give you a divorce as soon as possible.'

Shock hit her, and she sank back into the chair, all her new-found gladness vanishing like swallows at the first sign of frost. 'I thought you didn't believe in divorce,' she managed through stiff lips.

'I don't.' A muscle knotted in his jaw. 'But I should never have tried to force you to stay with me. You said we'd only make each other unhappy, and you were right.' Tonelessly he added, 'As of now you're free to go. You can leave as soon as you like without affecting Richard in any way.'

So it was all over. Even his obsession had died.

Or had it been an obsession? Remembering how certain Matt had been that Zan loved her, she took heart and said boldly, 'I don't intend to leave. At least not unless you *want* me to go.'

She heard the hiss of his indrawn breath, and just for a split-second glimpsed something in his face that gave her hope.

Then all expression was wiped away and he informed her coldly, 'I do want you to go. We can't live like this, tearing each other apart. And now there's no *need* for us to stay together...'

Clinging to that thread of hope, she changed tack. 'Tell me something... Why did you insist on me staying?'

'You know why.'

'Was it *only* because of the baby?' When he sat down heavily without answering, she persevered, 'Please Zan, tell me the truth.'

He hesitated so long she thought her appeal had failed, before admitting, 'I *wanted* you to stay. I couldn't bear the thought of losing you. The possibility that you might be pregnant came as a godsend. It provided a lever...

'I still thought, hoped, that you might be able to put the past behind you and trust me. I was wrong. All I can do now is say I'm sorry, and try to make amends.'

Careful of the words because the space between them was crammed with dangerous thoughts, she said quietly, 'Matt was here earlier. He asked what was wrong between us, and I told him.'

'He should have minded his own damn business,' Zan exploded angrily.

Clear aquamarine eyes met and held tawny in a level gaze. 'In a way it *was* his business. He admitted that *he'd* been Maya's lover; you'd merely been shielding him.'

There was a taut silence before Zan asked slowly, 'What do you intend to do about it?'

'Nothing. As far as I'm concerned it's over and done with. I wouldn't want Helen to be hurt.'

Zan sighed, then queried, 'You think I should have told you?'

She shook her head. 'I understand why you didn't.'

He sighed again. 'Try not to blame Matt too much; he was lonely and vulnerable... missing Helen. When he realised what a fool he'd been he made an effort to end things, but she was completely infatuated with him.

'I stepped in to try and head her off. Her phone calls were put through to me, and every time she came to the office I talked to her.

'It wasn't long before I realised she was emotionally unstable. I felt sorry for her, and several times when she was very low I took her out to lunch.

'Then one morning there was a slip-up and she managed to get through to Matt's office. She said she needed to see him and threatened to tell Helen about their affair if he didn't meet her.

'He panicked and promised to take her to dinner the next night. Then he came to me, worried to death.

'We agreed it would be better if he left the country for a while, and in less than two hours he was on a flight to the States. I'd promised to meet Maya in his place and make it clear that it really *was* all over, and telling Helen wouldn't alter a thing. That was the night you saw us together.

'It's strange how fate works. We were walking to our table when I glanced across the restaurant and met a woman's eyes. I found that ice, like fire, can burn. That cool, exquisite face seemed branded on my mind.'

As Annis's eyes widened, he added, 'This may sound hackneyed, but in that instant I knew you were the woman I'd been waiting all my life for.'

He got to his feet and began to pace. 'If the circumstances had been different I'd have come over and spoken to you there and then. But Maya was verging on the hysterical and threatening to cause a scene. When I looked your way again, you'd disappeared.

'Next day I returned to the restaurant and asked about you, but no one knew who you were. I couldn't believe I'd really lost you, and night after night for almost three weeks, I went back hoping to see you again...'

He moved to stand by the mantel, before resuming quietly, 'Then, as you know, I had to go over to the States. But still your face haunted me, and when I got home again I found myself looking for you, searching every crowd, chasing after any woman with flaxen hair in case it was you...'

Annis sat motionless, her eyes fixed on his face, filled with the deepest, most poignant emotion she'd ever known.

'Finally, when I'd lost all hope, I caught sight of you in Leighton's office. I was like a man possessed. I *had* to get to know you, to make you mine. I'm not usually so crass but I was terrified of losing you again.'

'Yet now you're telling me to go.'

He ran restless fingers through his shorn curls. 'Only because I can't live this way any longer.'

'But if we agreed to be friends?'

'I want a great deal more than friendship.'

'*Passionate* friends?'

'It's a tempting thought. But you see I don't want just passion. I want you to love me as deeply as I love you.'

Getting up, she went to him and put her hands flat against his chest. She felt his heartbeat accelerate beneath her palm as she said, 'I do love you. I've loved you for a long time but I...'

The rest of her words were lost, stifled by his mouth on hers.

They kissed like two people starving for one another, kissed until she felt breathless and her head reeled.

When she sagged against him, he sat down and took her on his lap, cradling her in his arms. 'Tell me again,' he ordered.

She glanced up at him from beneath long, gold-tipped lashes, and asked innocently, 'Tell you what?'

He pinched the lobe of her ear. 'That you love me. That you're mine.'

In response to what she recognised as real *need*, she put her arms around his neck, and, her cheek pressed against his, whispered, 'I'm yours, whilever I've got hands to hold you and lips to kiss you...'

His arms tightened until they almost crushed her ribs. 'I never thought I'd hear you say it.'

Her fingers following the curve of his jaw and tracing the cleft in his chin, she admitted, 'I think I started on the road to love that very first time I saw you with Maya...'

He grunted. 'But I've had to force you every step of the way.'

'Not *every* step,' she objected, remembering that night in San Francisco.

'Almost every step, you heartless witch. Don't you feel sorry for the way you've treated me?'

Seriously, she answered, 'I'm sorry I didn't believe you when you said you hadn't been Maya's lover.'

'It was asking a great deal,' he admitted. 'But the mere fact that you *wanted* to gave me hope... Then, after reading that damning note, I couldn't blame you for not believing me.'

'I just wish I had. It must have hurt you a lot.' She kissed him with a passion made all the deeper by regret.

'Kiss me like that every day for the rest of our lives and it will have been well worth it. And, speaking of the rest of our lives, how do you fancy a second honeymoon?'

'I don't feel as if I've had a first one yet, having wasted so much of it.'

'Hmm... Well, I suggest we rectify that immediately by having a double-length two-in-one. Where would you like to go?'

Unhesitatingly, she said, 'San Francisco... Hawaii...'

'Which?'

'Both. And if you want to make three people very happy...'

He lifted a quizzical brow. '*Three* people?'

'Matt was very concerned that things should be right between us. If you borrow Lani House again...'

Zan kissed her. 'Anything you say, my darling. So long as he doesn't want to come along.'

'He might prove useful...' she teased.

'*Useful*?'

'To give you a few tips... After all, he does have three children.'

Zan shook his head, eyes glinting. 'I don't need any tips. I shall go on the old maxim that practice makes perfect.'

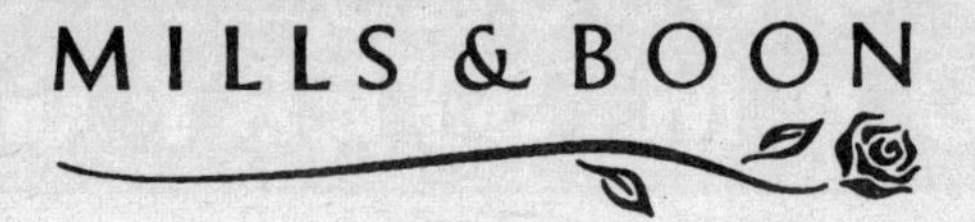

Next Month's Romances

Each month you can choose from a wide variety of romance with Mills & Boon. Below are the new titles to look out for next month.

THE HEAT OF PASSION	Lynne Graham
SWEET SINNER	Diana Hamilton
UNWANTED WEDDING	Penny Jordan
THE BRIDE IN BLUE	Miranda Lee
FAITH, HOPE AND MARRIAGE	Emma Goldrick
PS I LOVE YOU	Valerie Parv
PARTNER FOR LOVE	Jessica Hart
VOYAGE TO ENCHANTMENT	Rosemary Hammond
HOLLOW VOWS	Alexandra Scott
DISHONOURABLE SEDUCTION	Angela Wells
TEMPTATION ON TRIAL	Jenny Cartwright
TO TAME A TEMPEST	Sue Peters
POTENT AS POISON	Sharon Kendrick
SHORES OF LOVE	Alex Ryder
DANGEROUS ATTRACTION	Melinda Cross
PASSIONATE RETRIBUTION	Kim Lawrence

Available from WH Smith, John Menzies, Volume One, Forbuoys, Martins, Woolworths, Tesco, Asda, Safeway and other paperback stockists.